In Love With a Haunted House

Kate Goldman

In Love With a Haunted House

Published by Kate Goldman

Copyright © 2014 by Kate Goldman

ISBN 978-1-50051-624-6

First printing, 2014

www.KateGoldmanBooks.com

PRINTED IN THE UNITED STATES OF AMERICA

Dedication

I want to dedicate this book to my beloved husband, who makes every day in my life worthwhile. Thank you for believing in me when nobody else does, giving me encouragement when I need it the most, and loving me simply for being myself.

Table of Contents

Chapter 1

It was really over, Jim was never coming back.

Mallory knew that, and had known it almost from the moment she had come home to find him sitting in the living room with his hands folded across his knees in what she thought of as his "lecture" pose.

Anger replaced her melancholy. The bastard had packed, had his suitcases and other things removed before she had ever gotten home, and told her that the reason he had done so was to avoid, as he put it, any unpleasantness over the situation. He had known she could not fight against that, everything was already gone—what was there for her to fight for? She could not even try to stop him from packing, it was already finished.

He might as well have left a note rather than wait for her to get home to break the news to her in person. That would have been so like Jim! He never wanted to deal with anything that was remotely messy or complicated. He was always horrified by her tears, and distant enough to be living on another planet most of the time. Why had she never seen that before that moment? Why had she simply allowed her own feelings to overwrite her good sense?

Mallory wove her way through the hastily packed boxes that held her possessions. It gave her a slight spiteful satisfaction to know that Jim would have been horrified by that haphazard packing.

Not that she had had much choice—she was rapidly running out of money and if she did not get out of the apartment today she was going to have sign another year's lease, which she could not afford.

She looked out the window. At first only her own reflection stared back: pale oval face, large green eyes and high cheekbones all surrounded by a mass of curly reddish-gold hair, but then the view below came into focus.

Mallory's heart twisted. Living on this coveted section of real estate in Chicago had been an outward sign of their success—hers and Jim's. The lake stretched blue and serene dozens of stories below her high-rise condo apartment. She could see wind-fattened sails on the boats cruising slowly on the placid waters, and the narrow ribbon of road that ran around the lake.

Once she had taken Jim for a ride through the grittier parts of the city simply to show him how much better they had it than so many others, why they had so much to be grateful for, and he had not spoken to her for an entire week except to inform her, quite frostily, that he had no intention of allowing her to get him murdered.

They had never left their own neighborhood again after that.

Her anger faded and tears began. It seemed like her moods swung in every direction lately like a pendulum without any steadying weight. Her cheeks were soaked before she could wipe those tears away and so was the windowsill. That was probably going to ruin the wood.

Mallory turned back around and gave the boxes an almost puzzled look. Was she really doing this? Was she really going home after nearly eight years away?

It seemed that she was. And it was hardly the triumphant homecoming she had always imagined.

Mallory had come to Chicago with ambition to spare. She had taken college courses while still in high school as well as having obtained a degree in accounting right after. She was intelligent, willing to work long hours and she wanted to see a big city far away from her small hometown.

She had gotten a job offer from Logitechnics and had jumped on it. Everything had just seemed to fall into place. She had moved into a tiny little apartment and gone to work. She had met Jim, who was a university professor, and after a year they had moved in together.

The next year they had moved into this apartment and things had just coasted along. Until a year ago when they had begun saving for both their wedding and a house of their own.

Mallory knew she should have seen the writing on the wall but she had been nearing twenty-eight, ready to settle down, ready for children, and she had honestly thought that after all the years she and that asshole had together he was too.

The very same day she had come home already in tears, because she had been handed a notice informing her that the company had been bought out and that she was one of the employees whose job could be done cheaper through outsourcing, she had come home to find him parked on the sofa waiting to break the news to her that the engagement was off and he was moving out.

The days afterward had drifted by. She had spent nearly three days in bed, curled around cartons of rocky road and mint chocolate chip, wiping her tears on her increasingly dingy sheets and watching romance films on Netflix.

Mallory had not even been able to talk to Jim. He had moved and not given her a forwarding address (but he had put one in at the post office nearly two weeks before, just one more example of how cold-hearted he was) and he had changed his phone number.

It was the beginning of summer so he would not be at the university and when she called up the hotel where they usually spent a week every summer she was met with a disapproving silence, a cleared throat and the suggestion that she check the hotel's policy on giving out personal information on its guests.

Mallory might have stayed right there in bed for a month or more if she had not run out of both ice cream and peanut butter. Not to mention being jarred completely out of her stupor by the rude wake-up call from the building manager.

The manager had informed her that she needed to be reapproved for the apartment and that if she did qualify to stay she would have to fork over a hefty sum of fees and rental money.

Mallory had her severance package and her half of the money that she and Jim had been saving for the nuptials and the house. She could have afforded maybe six months in the apartment, the rent was staggering—almost four thousand a month—and accompanied by fees and other incidental charges.

Mallory wanted to stick it out—to try to find a job and hang on there in Chicago but she knew that was not possible. Everyone that had been downsized was desperate for a job and their numbers only added to the count of people already unemployed in the city.

Her mother had provided the solution almost by accident. Mallory had not wanted to answer the phone, all she needed was to listen to her mother try to cheer her up. She knew she meant well; it was just that Cara, her mother, always saw the bright side of things—even when they were so dark that they looked downright desolate. Mallory didn't know how she managed to do that and at that moment she didn't really care either, but she answered the phone anyway. She knew Cara would just keep calling back until she did, so she might as well get it over with.

"You are never going to believe what happened," Cara said as soon as her daughter picked up the phone.

"Somebody had twins?"

"No, although Louise Roberts, do you remember Louise? looks like she might have triplets but if you ask me that is all the ice cream she's been eating. Anyway, Ms. Lewis died."

"Who?" Mallory's head ached but that was not an uncommon thing when she spoke to her mother.

"Ms. Lewis, the one that owned Gray Oaks Manor."

Gray Oaks Manor. The house that sat next door to Mallory's childhood home. It was a tall and almost imposing Victorian structure with stained-glass windows on the third floor and giant elm and oak trees, most of them covered with Spanish moss, shielding it from casual view.

"I didn't know she was still alive."

"I don't think anyone did really, poor soul. To be honest I had almost forgotten she was over there. The last few years she barely even came outside. It wasn't until her lawn service noticed she had not paid her bill this month that they got curious and knocked on her door."

"Oh my God, you're not about to tell me that she was dead for months before they figured it out, are you?"

"Oh no. It's even stranger than that. When one of the men from her lawn service knocked on the door she opened it, wearing a wedding dress. Not just any wedding dress either, it had to be sixty or seventy years old and when they tried to talk to her she just kept saying that she did not have time to talk, she was getting ready for her wedding."

"That poor old thing. Didn't her fiancé die or something?"

Cara said, "Yes, in World War II, I think, or maybe Korea. I have no idea really, and I don't think she did anymore either. She's been senile for years, you know."

Mallory said, "Everyone knew that she was senile, but she still had enough money that nobody wanted to put her in a home."

"Yes, if she had lived in a tiny little house on the other side of town somebody would've simply snatched her out of her house a long time ago and put her away. But that's not why I was calling you, well, actually it is why I was calling you.

"You always loved Gray Oaks, and you always wanted to buy it. Well, here's your chance. It's going dirt cheap, apparently she left the outside of the house up to her lawn service and the guy who came around to clean out the gutters, but the inside is a real mess."

Mallory asked, "Mom, have you lost your mind?"

Cara replied, "No, but if I did, don't tell anybody. I want to stay in my home until I die too. Did I tell you how she died?"

Mallory shook her head, the whole conversation was going right off the rails into some uncharted territory that she was not sure she even wanted to try to navigate at the moment. "No, you didn't."

"Well, it seems that the guy who owns the lawn service decided she needed some help. I mean you can't blame the guy; she was flitting around in a falling-apart wedding dress asking him if he had seen her cake pans, so he called an ambulance.

"The ambulance driver showed up and decided that she was all the way off her rocker and that she needed to be hospitalized but when they tried to take her out of the house she told them that if they took her away she would be late for her own wedding and that she wasn't going to have that.

"They got her all the way to the door and I do mean all the way to the door. Before her feet crossed the threshold she grabbed ahold of the door frame and shouted out 'I do, I do' and fell over dead."

Mallory's mouth sagged open to her breastbone. Ms. Lewis had always been odd, to say the least, and it was no secret that everyone in town thought that her house was haunted although Mallory had never seen any evidence of that.

"Mom, you do know you're trying to talk me into buying a house where a woman just dropped dead in the doorway?"

"Yes, I do know that, but think about it—you could afford it. Isn't that the most important thing?"

"I don't even know what to say to that, Mom."

"Say that you'll come home. Then ask me for the name of the person selling the place, you better hurry up, though, if you want to buy it. You know half the town has been dying to get their hands on that property."

"Mom, what would I do in Golden?"

"Well, what are you doing in Chicago?"

Ouch. "That's a little unfair. You know I'm trying to find a job."

"I know you're up there eating your own misery. You can get a job here, John Markham has a just expanded his advertising agency and he could use a hand. Not only that, there are a lot of businesses here in town that could use a good accountant; you could set up your own business."

"Mom, that is so risky."

"It seems to me that getting a job with another company that might lay you off is pretty risky."

Mallory could see no way to argue with that. Now, just a few days later here she was: packed, ready to go, and trying to figure out if she had temporarily lost her mind or just fallen victim to one of her mom's plots.

It didn't really matter. She could not afford to stay in Chicago; she couldn't afford it financially, or emotionally. Jim had done a number on her and maybe it would do him some good to know that he had lost her.

That stopped her in her tracks. Was that what this was all about? Was she hoping that she would get back to Golden and Jim would come running after her? She hoped not, surely she was not that big of a fool.

Chapter 2

Blake spotted the road that he was supposed to turn on, hooked a finger around the truck's turn signal and made the curve. The old truck rattled and groaned as he did so and he wondered, a trifle uneasily, if the entire rear end was about to fall out from under the damn thing. It would not surprise him at all.

The street was a surprisingly wide avenue, sidewalks on each side were gray ribbons interrupting lush green lawns, many of them with fanciful arrangements of flowers and even fountains.

Most of the houses on the street were recorded in the historical preservation society's register. Some of them were small, almost boxy, while others were large two- and three- storied affairs. He spotted two Greek Revival houses complete with Doric columns, and a tiny little Cape Cod style cottage that was so out of place it drew the eye, stealing its neighbors' thunder quite effectively.

None of the houses, however, could hold a candle to Gray Oaks. He pulled into the tree-lined driveway and cut the engine. He sat back in the seat, surveying the house before him, and a smile curved his full lips.

Gray Oaks had been built in the 1850s by a former sea captain turned farmer. At one time its grounds had taken up over 400 acres but now only a single acre remained. Still, a house sitting on an acre in the middle of the city was hard to find. One with a history like the history that Gray Oaks boasted was nearly impossible to find.

Blake swung his lean body out of the truck. His jeans clung to his long muscled legs and tight narrow waist. His T-shirt showed the width of his chest and the wiry lean muscles in his arms. He tilted his trim frame against the hot truck and leaned his face back to the sun.

This was his house. He was going to buy it even if it killed him, and nobody was going to stop him from doing it.

Mallory, pulling into the driveway of her own house next door to Gray Oaks, saw the good-looking man leaning against the truck over at Gray Oaks. Assuming he was the real estate agent, she cut off her own engine and got out of her car. Her mother was not home from work yet and while the ride down from Chicago had been long and really boring, it had not been excessively tiring so she decided to go over and speak to the man.

As she got closer she could tell that her initial impression had been right, he was good-looking and he got even more good-looking with every step. The sun, coming through the trees, placed bright lemony dapples of light on his face, emphasizing the good bone structure beneath his tanned skin.

"Hello."

Blake's light blue eyes flew open and he jerked away from the truck like he'd been shot. For a single moment his heart jackhammered against his chest walls as he remembered all the old stories about the house being haunted. It only took a second for him to realize that this woman facing him was flesh and blood. And what flesh and blood! She was utterly beautiful, despite the dark shadows below her eyes and the drooping of her shoulders.

"I didn't mean to startle you, I'm sorry." She had a beautiful contralto voice: low and almost smoky. It reminded him of the voice of an old-time jazz singer, he could listen to her talk for hours. "I was pulling up and I saw you over here so I thought I would come over and introduce myself. I'm Mallory."

She tilted her head as she spoke, and his eyes followed that movement to see the car parked in the driveway of the house next door. So, she was his new neighbor or she would be as soon as he finished buying the house. That was yet another selling point.

He extended a hand to her and Mallory took it. She could feel the calluses on his fingertips and palms, the

13

strength within his grip, and a blush heated her face. She became tongue-tied for a moment and couldn't think of what to say. When she finally did manage to stutter something out it was, "I'm really looking forward to living here at Gray Oaks."

His gaze sharpened. His grip also tightened, his head tilted to one side. A rich, warm baritone voice came out of his mouth as he asked, "What are you talking about? I'm buying this house."

Mallory blinked several times. "No, no. I thought you were the real estate agent, that's why I came over here to say hello. Who are you?"

"I'm Blake Hunter."

He said that like she should recognize his name. For some reason that irritated her a little. "And?"

"And I'm buying this house. I'm waiting for the real estate agent now."

"That's impossible! I drove all the way here from Chicago to meet the agent today."

"It might be a little hard to live in this house if you live in Chicago."

Mallory glared at him. How could a man be so handsome and yet so irritating? And how dare that agent set up two appointments in the same day? The least she could have done was tell Mallory that she would have other people looking at the house! She yanked her hand away from his and said, "I'm moving home."

"Well, I hope you have a secondary choice. I'm not giving up this house."

"Who says you'll get it?"

Blake said, "Listen, I think we're getting off on the wrong foot here. I'm just as upset as you are about this double booking of appointments. It's just bad business but then again, given the fact that a house like this hasn't been on the market in, I don't know, a dozen years or more, I can see why she did it."

Mallory asked, "You aren't from here, are you?"

Blake grimaced. He'd heard that a lot since he'd first come to Golden. "No, I'm originally from Atlanta."

Mallory nodded. "I should've known, not that you're not from here but that Louise would pull a stunt like this. You should have known her in high school—she double charged for the candy bars all of us on the cheerleading team were supposed to sell to raise money for a competition and pocketed the extra profit."

That amused Blake so much that he had to suppress a grin. "She sounds enterprising."

Mallory had to laugh at that even though she didn't want to. "That's one way to put it, yes. So if you aren't from here how did you hear about Gray Oaks being for sale?"

His face closed like a fist. All expression left it and she could tell she had asked the question that he was not going to answer. When he spoke his tone was completely impassive. "I found it on a search engine."

He was lying! But why? Before Mallory could try to make sense of that, Louise's sporty little red convertible pulled up at the curb. She climbed out of the car and Blake let out a whistle. "Do you think we should go give her a hand?"

"My mom says she eats too much ice cream." Now why had she said that? Maybe because as soon as she had seen Blake looking at Louise she had been smitten by jealousy although she was not sure why. She did not even know the guy.

"Thanks for telling me. I was going to try to win her over by asking her when she was due." The smile lurking around the corners of his mouth made him even more attractive. Mallory's heart gave a strange little flutter; one that she tried to dismiss as gas from the chili dog she'd eaten from a gas station on her way into town.

"She's due in three weeks. Don't let her use that to jack up the price on you. She will if she thinks she can."

"Are you conceding defeat?"

She gave him a smile through clenched teeth. "No, I'm giving you a fighting chance."

"I appreciate it."

"I'm sure you do."

Louise's obviously pregnant body was covered head to toe in pastel linen that looked like it was stretched to the breaking point. She wore a giant floppy hat to shade her pale face and she waved at them merrily as she tripped along from the sidewalk to the driveway in her sensible little flat ballet shoes.

As she came abreast of them she cried out, "Dear heavens, it is hotter than the hinges of hell! We should get inside before we all melt!" She gave Blake an appraising stare, then let her eyes run over Mallory so quickly that there was no doubt in Mallory's mind she had just been dismissed.

Blake immediately took Louise's arm, tossing Mallory a nasty little wink as he did so. Mallory would have stomped her foot in sheer frustration if she had not known exactly how childish that would look. She wound up falling behind them as they went up the flagstone walk and onto the wide and gracious front porch.

Louise kept up a steady stream of chatter, pointing out obvious things such as the porch, the long and gracious windows and the sturdy oak of the front door as they went in. Once in the foyer, Louise's babble became even more annoying and Mallory would have liked to wander off alone but she was afraid to. There was no telling what this charming stranger might get up to with Louise while she was out of sight. Not that it looked like Louise could get up to much; it looked as if she would barely be able get from the living room to the large dining room, past it and then to the kitchen without passing out or giving birth.

The staircase ran off the foyer, arcing gracefully in an almost semicircle pattern before it attached to a landing which ran down the entire length of the second floor. Louise paused at the staircase, one hand on the banister and both feet on the floor below.

"Sorry, kids, I'm afraid this is as far as I can go. You will have to show yourselves the upstairs but be warned, it's a bit of a mess."

The whole house was a bit of a mess and that was an understatement. Many of the floors were gouged, the hardwood broken and splintered. The wallpaper had peeled away from the walls and had never been repaired. Some of the crown molding was broken and the stairs looked decidedly rickety.

The kitchen had been orderly, but the appliances were all practically ancient and of a revolting avocado green color that had made Mallory jerk backwards as if she were a vampire suddenly threatened with sunlight. Blake had seen that and given her a bright tooth-baring grin that was almost frightening in its whiteness.

"Not a fan of bile, I take it?"

Her glare would have melted lesser men but Blake was immune, it seemed. He was also not a gentleman. He looked at the stairs and back at her and said, "Ladies first."

"Are you hoping to get a good look at my bottom or are you hoping I'll just crash through a stair and save you the trouble and expense of outbidding me?"

Louise gasped at Mallory's words but Blake merely grinned. "I'll take whatever I can get."

His reply left her flummoxed. He was the most impossible man! "You go first."

He bounded up the stairs and grinned down at her from a landing. Where was a falling chandelier when she needed one? She went up the stairs a lot more slowly, testing each one to make sure it would hold her weight even though she knew he was watching, and amused by her reluctance.

The upstairs was a mess. Dust had collected in every corner and the floors, while not as seriously damaged as they were downstairs, needed a good cleaning and some fresh coatings of polyurethane.

The bedrooms were furnished and the furnishings were good but somewhat worn out. One bedroom made Mallory stop and stare. This had to be Ms. Lewis's room: the bed was high and covered with a vast array of hand-sewn quilts. The pictures on the walls all showed a handsome man captured in black-and-white and sepia tones, his uniform fitting his trim and lean body perfectly.

Was this the man that had died and left her all alone? The story was that she had never gotten over her fiancé's tragic death and had pined away for him for the rest of her life. Was that true? Could someone love someone else so much that everything just sort of stopped in their own lives after their beloved died?

"Yes, that was exactly how it was. When he died over there in the war everything just stopped here, like a clock whose hands had gotten stuck."

Mallory's head jerked around. Had she just heard someone speak? She looked around, trying to see if there was a curtain flipping against a wall or anything else that could have made a sound that would have been similar to a voice speaking, but she saw nothing.

How silly of her, she was letting old ghost stories bother her. Well, those and this hunk of a man whose jeans were currently stretched nice and tight over his firm round buttocks as he bent to inspect a baseboard. It should be illegal for a man to wear jeans that tight! Or to have a butt like that, he was probably one of those guys that spent four hours a day in the gym and four more in front of his mirror. That uncharitable thought made her instantly ashamed. He wanted the same house she wanted, that was no reason to be so unkind.

Blake was trying very hard not to pay attention to Mallory. That was easier said than done though since everything about her was incredibly appealing. It was not just her body, either, she had a sense of humor and she was sharp as a tack; that was obvious. Other men might be a sucker for breasts and a well-shaped ass, not that he was immune to those things, but what he really was, was a sucker for smart. And Mallory was smart as a whip, and not afraid to let that show. Too many women hid their intelligence, hoping to keep men from finding them intimidating. In Blake's opinion any man intimidated by a smart woman did not deserve one.

"Take it easy," he told himself. "First off she's not looking like she wants to be friends and what's more—what would she say if she knew your history?"

That threw a little cold water on his growing attraction, but not much. And nothing was dimming his desire for the house. He took a step closer to her and said, "So you grew up next door to here, huh?"

"I thought I recognized you, dearie."

She had definitely heard a voice!

"Are you okay?"

Mallory looked at Blake. "What?"

"Are you okay? You look a little pale."

Of course she was pale; someone invisible was talking to her! "It's hot up here."

"There doesn't seem to be any good air-conditioning up here. Maybe you should consider that when you are bidding."

"Nice try, buddy," Mallory said.

Blake opened his mouth to say something in return but before he could he was shoved, literally, across the room and into a large wardrobe. The doors of the wardrobe slammed shut, but not before Mallory caught a glimpse of his shocked face and wide-open mouth.

She was tempted to just leave him there to suffer but after he began to pound on the doors with both fists and yell some very indelicate words she took pity on him. She opened the doors and peered in at him, asking quite sweetly, "Are you okay? You look a little pale."

Blake climbed out of the wardrobe. He wanted to ask her if she had seen what had just happened, but on the other hand he was determined to pretend as if suddenly flying across the room and into a large piece of furniture was a common occurrence.

That could not have just happened! There had to be some kind of explanation for it, maybe the floor had a slippery spot and he had lost his balance and just crashed into the damn thing. He managed to dust off his hands and knees slowly and deliberately while she tried, with very little success, to wipe that smirk right off her pretty face.

"Yoo-hoo! Are you two kids okay up there?"

"Was she always that annoying?"

Mallory grinned at him. "Worse. She's actually mellowed according to what my mom says."

"Does your mom spend much time with her?"

"Not if she can help it." Mallory was trying to pretend that she had not just seen him being hurtled across the room and into a wardrobe. In the entire span of her childhood she had never seen one thing in this house that would make her suspect it was haunted. Then again she never actually been inside the house, either, she had always just admired it from her bedroom window or her side yard.

"He deserved a little bit of a takedown."

The voice was back, and she was willing to bet that it actually belonged to Ms. Lewis. But what would Ms.

23

Lewis be doing haunting her own haunted house? The truth was probably far simpler and less extraordinary. She had just driven almost 14 hours straight while slugging back those horrible little five-hour energy drinks along with oversized cups of coffee. Not to mention she had spent almost an entire week sucking down sugar and nothing else, her body and brain were probably just reacting to some kind of withdrawal or sugar shock.

"We should probably go down before she tries to climb the stairs." Blake looked at Mallory, and then said, "You have a little smudge of dirt right there."

He leaned close to her, his finger coming out to stroke lightly across her cheek. His touch made her shiver, and not in a bad way. She had never experienced the sensations that were swirling through her right then—she wanted to kiss him! She wanted to lean against his chest and see if it was a strong as it looked, and she wanted to put her face in his faded shirt and see if it smelled like cologne like she suspected that it did.

What was wrong with her? She had just been dumped by a man that she was supposed to marry and spend her entire life with, the last thing on earth she needed was to start running after this one.

Chapter 3

Cara looked up at her daughter as she paced the living room floor. "So Louise had more than one potential buyer?"

Mallory said, "Yes. I should've known, she always was one to hedge her bets. Now tell me again how she wound up being the one to sell that house."

"Well, apparently there was a fight between some of the descendants. There was talk about there being an…ahem…illegitimate heir. Some say that old Ms. Lewis had quite a few secrets, a kid born out of wedlock among them."

"That's just crazy. She never even left the house!"

"Oh I know, can you imagine? Who would she have had a child with anyway? The grocery delivery boy or her lawn service guy?"

Mallory asked, "Is that same man that used to cut her grass still cutting it? Because the last time I saw him he weighed about three hundred pounds."

"Maybe he got all sweaty cutting grass and came in for a drink of water, maybe she just couldn't resist him."

"Mom, you read way too many romance novels."

"I do." Her laughter tinkled out to the living room. "Ever since your father left I guess that's pretty much where I get my fill of romantic enjoyment."

That was still a sore spot for Mallory. She had been completely unable to believe that her parents were getting divorced after twenty-one years of marriage but they had. Her father had said that he was simply unhappy, and that her mother was, too, and while things had seemed amicable on the surface Mallory often wondered if they really were.

The truth was her mother actually did seem even more ridiculously cheerful, not that she ever had seemed depressed. She did have that sunny disposition after all. On an impulse Mallory asked, "Mom, do you ever miss having Dad around?"

"Of course I do, we were together for a very long time and it's hard not to miss somebody when you're used to them being around."

"How do you know you don't love him anymore?"

"Because I don't. Mallory, I hope you're not thinking that maybe you can pull off some plot to get your father and me back together. That's never going to happen, we're both very happy."

She decided to change the subject. "I saw pictures in Ms. Lewis's bedroom today. They were of a guy in uniform. Like, a military uniform. Maybe that's the guy that died and left her all alone."

"Maybe she was just a sucker for a guy in uniform."

Mallory threw her hands up in the air. "Mom, you're impossible!"

"Yes, but think of it. Wouldn't it be interesting if she actually did have an unclaimed child running around somewhere? It would be almost like a soap opera right here on our very own street."

Mallory gave up. When her mom got to thinking about things like that there was no stopping her, the best thing she could do was simply drop the subject. Even if Ms. Lewis had had a child, it would be as old as Cara by now.

**

In his small motel room Blake was thinking about Mallory. He had tried to turn his thoughts elsewhere ever since he'd gotten back to the shabby little place, but given that the decor looked like a drunk interior designer with a vendetta against the motel had been allowed to run amok inside the rooms, and the fact that the TV didn't work, there was precious little else to occupy his mind.

So, she had grown up next door to Gray Oaks. He wondered if she'd ever seen any ghosts there. What was he thinking? There was no such thing as ghosts, and everyone who said that the house was haunted was either just another gossip or buying into the hysteria.

Or did he really believe that? Something had happened today, he had felt something push him across that floor and into that wardrobe whether he wanted to admit it or not. It had been the oddest feeling, and that strange slide across the floor had felt like he was being pushed by a strong wind. Right before the wardrobe had closed he had thought he had seen a woman standing behind Mallory.

That was insane, of course. Ghosts did not exist. He was a grown man, not some terrified high school kid who had listened to one too many campfire stories. He had to have slipped on the floor. Maybe he'd been so distracted by Mallory's mouth he hadn't even noticed her hands coming up to push him.

Of course, it would have been impossible not to notice anybody pushing him that fast and that hard. It had been a hell of a push. He'd gone flying across the floor like he was on skates and the floor was covered in oil.

I am overthinking this, he thought. That did not give him any comfort, and it did not stop his thoughts either. Okay, so he was overthinking it. So be it. He'd had a lot on his mind ever since he had learned that Gray Oaks would be put up for sale.

Shannon Lewis had not left any direct relatives, or so they claimed. That wasn't true — and Blake should know, he was her grandson.

Not that anybody on her side of the family would've ever claimed him. They had been mortified apparently back in the day when she had gotten pregnant with his father. She'd been banking on marrying his grandfather, but he had the bad manners to get himself killed in the war, leaving her not only pregnant but single. In those days women who bore children out of wedlock were not looked upon well, and her family had hoped that she might come to her senses and wed at some point.

He often wished he could've met her, but she did not want to know him. She had never wanted to know his father either and in a way he could not blame her. She had spent several months stashed away in a small summer house belonging to his paternal grandparents. As soon as she had borne his father, her own family had come and taken her away, leaving his father with his grandparents.

Blake often wondered how badly that desertion had cut his father. George Hunter Jr. was a very quiet man, one who did not do anything lightly. He had married very late in life, so that by the time Blake was in high school he was already in his 60s.

He had never spoken about his mother, not even when Blake had pressed him. When Blake had gone to his grandparents, who were already reaching the end of their lives by then, they had told him that Shannon Lewis was as rich as she was crazy, and she was very rich.

It had been his grandmother who had told them all about Gray Oaks and its storied history. It had begun as a sea captain's house, a sea captain who had fallen so completely in love with a woman that he'd been willing to give up his ship and his sailing career for her.

He built a house and named it Gray Oaks for the long strands of Spanish moss that hung from the giant trees that shaded the drive. They had no sooner married and had children, settling into the life of well-to-do farmers, than rebellion and unrest began to break out all across the South.

It was rumored that the Underground Railroad had a station there in an outbuilding, and then after the war the house passed into the hands of a niece who had taken it into her head to be an actress in an age when actresses were often the subject of much scandal.

The actress had thrown huge parties, and apparently had a really good time. Her many lovers had come and gone. And she had three children, none of them legitimate. One of her children was one of the earliest mobsters in Chicago and after his fortune was assured he moved back to town and set up residence in the house after his mother died.

That man was Shannon Lewis's father. Perhaps it was no surprise that Shannon was headstrong and stubborn, that she wanted what she wanted and she had no intention of settling for anything else. What she had wanted was one George Hunter, even though his family found her to be entirely unsuitable.

Blake sometimes wondered if Shannon didn't come to see his father simply because she was afraid his grandparents would not allow it. He supposed it really didn't matter why, all he knew is that there were only two relatives left in the family: him and a distant cousin who wanted to sell the house as quickly as possible and take off with the money. Blake had no issue with that, except he wanted the house.

He didn't really even know why, it just seemed to him that it was the right place for him.

Blake had grown up outside Atlanta and Golden, 100 miles to the south, was a thriving and bustling midsize city. He had often driven down to Golden, once he got his license, and spent hours just circling the block around his grandmother's house.

Sometimes he would park his car at a nearby grocery store or park and walk the neighborhood in which his grandmother lived. So many of the houses were beautiful, imposing and tall, but none of them were as beautiful as Gray Oaks to him.

As soon as his father had informed him that Shannon had died Blake knew that he had to have that house. He was going to have that house. Nothing was going to stop him from getting it. He had known who Shannon's lawyer was because his grandparents remembered what firm she had used and the only difference between that firm then and now was that now the grandson had taken over the family business.

Blake had informed the lawyer that he wanted the house and that Ms. Lewis was his grandmother so he had every right to it and if he wasn't in the will that was fine. He would buy the property outright. Then, the fighting had begun.

Blake had to admit that was probably the biggest mistake he had ever made. He should have just waited until it went on the market and tried to buy it that way but he had never considered that his distant cousin might be one of the greediest human beings on the planet.

He was, though, and he was determined not to give Blake anything, not even a crumb off the floor of the old place. Thankfully he did want to sell, however, and although the price he named originally was far too high, Blake was sure that he would come down, especially when the appraisal on the house went through and came up with a depressingly low number.

The place had been kept up on the outside but Shannon Lewis had not allowed anyone inside in decades so nobody had known the extent of the repairs that would be needed. They had made Blake's heart sink a little as well but he was a good carpenter and he had worked on several restoration projects in his line of work. He was confident he could do most of the work himself and do it well.

Now if he could just stop thinking about Mallory…

**

The next day dawned clear and bright and Blake woke up feeling very optimistic. That feeling changed when his phone rang and Louise said, in her bright chirp of a voice, "I hate to tell you but Lonny Lewis just took a carload of the historical society folks over to the house. He stopped by here to pick up the keys since he only had the one set. I thought I would just give you a heads-up."

Damn!

Blake was not a fool. Louise was not telling him that out of the kindness of her heart, she was hoping to twist a higher bid out of him now that he knew the house was in danger of being gobbled up by the society.

He didn't have much more money to play with, though, so his only hope was to make the house as unattractive as possible to the society

He hung up and grabbed his jeans off the floor, sliding them over his narrow hips and donning a T-shirt and his boots before grabbing his keys and heading out. He drove quickly and arrived at the house just in time to see Mallory in a heated discussion with his distant cousin.

As soon as Mallory had seen Mrs. Williams and her cronies climbing out of the long black car she had known what was going on. That damned Lonnie Lewis was trying to sell Gray Oaks to the historical society!

She marched over there, forgetting that she was wearing her pajamas: a set of pink lace-trimmed shorts and a matching camisole top and nothing else. The women had seen her coming and stared at Mallory, scandalized—or at least pretending to be. Mallory had not noticed them, or the fact that Lonnie's beady little eyes were glued to her erect nipples, clearly visible through the thin top.

"Just what the hell are you doing, Lonnie?"

Lonnie Lewis looked like he had a terminal case of intestinal worms. He was skinny with a curve in his spine that was due not to medical issues but his utter refusal to stand upright. He had hair that had gone

In Love With a Haunted House

thin in patches, giving him the look of a mangy dog, and his teeth were a decidedly yellow color from the cigarettes he always had planted between his thin lips.

He gave her a long look. "Well, Mallory, I heard you were back in town. You look very good too." His eyes raked her figure and she had the urge to strangle him. In high school he had been the guy who was always sneaking into the girls' locker room and giving girls little squeezes on their backsides when he thought nobody was looking.

At the time his parents had still been alive and what they had lacked in actual money they made up for in power so most had ignored his antics but Mallory never had. She had once cracked him right across his face for grabbing her in an entirely inappropriate manner and he had never forgotten it, or forgiven her.

"I asked you a question."

"I don't believe it's any of your business. My great-great aunt left me this place and I can do whatever the hell I want to with it."

"You pompous little ass! She left you nothing! She left it to your folks so it went to you by proxy. I'm sure she would have hated to see those stuck-up old crones walking through her door!"

Blake heard that last and he had to stifle a laugh. Mallory was quite a sight angry, hell, she was quite a

35

sight at any time. That camisole and shorts set she was wearing was enough to kill a man too. Her legs stuck out of the bottom of the shorts: tanned and long and gorgeous, and her breasts were almost visible below the pink material...he had better stop looking or he was going to have more to worry about than losing the house. He was going to be worried about losing his dignity.

Mallory groaned inwardly when she saw Blake approaching. Of course he would show up now, just when everything else was going so badly. He didn't look like he had wasted any time getting there either— his hair was sleep rumpled and there was a definite crease down on one side of his face from either a pillow or a sheet.

She didn't like where that train of thought was headed so she turned her attention back to the hapless Lonnie and added a few more choice words about his lineage and his looks to her diatribe.

Blake grasped her upper arm gently. He was amused but he was also a little surprised by her passion. Did Gray Oaks really mean so much to her then and if it did, why?

"Listen, Mallory, while that outfit is certainly enjoyable for the rest of us I think it might be best if you changed out of it, at least for now."

Her face flamed. How dare he tell her what to wear! Okay, so she was practically naked in the street, but still…she favored him with a withering glare. "Don't think you can talk this piece of crap into taking your side, he is the greediest thing alive."

"Oh dear," Lonnie said in an exaggerated drawl, "look who rode to the rescue, my dear estranged cousin."

Cousin? Had Lonnie just said cousin? She gave Blake a baleful stare and he said, with a shrug of his broad shoulders, "Don't blame me. I can't help biology. And I am not here to rescue this turd.

"How about breakfast after you get dressed?"

Mallory stared at him, surely he was joking! He had to be! He was Lonnie's cousin, he was after her house and…his jeans were still indecently tight, stretched across his lean hips and fitting snugly into the fork between his hard muscular thighs…

"Yes, okay." Had she just said that? It was like she had been hypnotized by the gleam of the rivets on his front pockets.

"Breakfast. Just don't expect me to cook it. I'm a lousy cook."

"I'm sure you have other charms," Lonnie sneered.

Mallory interrupted Blake's glower with a calm, "I see you still have a scar from the last time you messed with me, Lonnie. Better think of a nicer way to phrase things or you might end up with another one."

"That's a threat!"

Blake said, "I didn't hear a threat, I just heard her tell you to stop being such a pervert."

Mallory would have laughed if things were not so surreal and spiraling even further out of control with each passing second. She turned and walked to her own house, uncomfortably aware of the breeze blowing against her mostly exposed thighs.

Lonnie gave Blake a yellow-toothed grin. "I guess you better come up with some extra money, cuz. It seems the society has been after this house for years."

There wasn't any extra money and they both knew it. Blake turned his attention back to the house, wondering if there was anything at all he could do to help get the women in there out of there. Where was a good ghost when you needed one?

Mallory was thinking the same thing. Her bedroom window faced the house and she stared at it as she yanked on a pair of jeans and a pretty blue silk sleeveless blouse, ran a hasty comb through her locks and dashed on a bit of mascara and lip gloss.

It was odd, she had not really wanted the house. Not since she was a little kid dreaming about owning it, anyway; it had simply been the best solution to a problem. But now, now that other people wanted it, she just had to have it. She wasn't sure what that said about her.

She said, "Ms. Lewis, you didn't want those old biddies that you never liked in your house when you were alive. If you don't want them in your house now, you better do something about it."

She turned away from the window and went out the front door, crossing the yard to meet with Blake, who still stood under the alley of trees next to Lonnie. The front door burst open and the women came out. All of them were making a rather undignified and hurried exit.

One was not just in a hurry, she was actually running like her feet were on fire and her butt was catching, as the rather quaint little Southern saying went. She went so fast her wig flew off, hovered in the air like a weird little bat and then it landed at the feet of another woman, who gave it a hurried little kick as she went past it.

Lonnie stuttered out, "Ladies…ladies…What are you doing?"

Blake said, "It looks like the historical society has become the hysterical society. I doubt they want the house, Lonnie."

The tires squealing as the women left seemed to emphasize that point. Lonnie was not one to let a minor setback sway him, though. "No worries. I got a developer coming tomorrow. He wants to tear the place down, put in a little apartment house complete with swimming pool and a gym for the residents."

He swaggered off. Blake and Mallory stared at each other and then Mallory said, "That is it, then. I could fight the society if I had to but a developer, no way. I can't afford any other house in the neighborhood or much of anywhere else to be honest. I hope you really want it."

Sympathy welled up in him and an affection he had not expected. "What I want is breakfast. What do you think made those women run so fast? A rat maybe?"

"You'd think if they were frightened of rats they would have spooked at the sight of Lonnie."

"You have a point there."

Neither of them wanted to say what they were thinking. The ghost of Gray Oaks had struck again.

**

Well, they are right although they're wrong too. The only person who haunted this house all those years was me and I'm still here. I keep hoping you're going to show up, George, and tell me everything is going to be okay and that you forgive me for doing what I did to our son. I hope he had a good life, he would never have had one here and we both know that.

My family's reputation was bad enough, I didn't want our child to be born out of wedlock too, I saw my own aunts and father deal with that stigma and it was never pretty. Times sure have changed, though, hardly any child is born in wedlock these days.

Oh well. Did you see that silly woman lose her wig? That was the funniest thing I've seen in a dozen years.

I really like that girl, the one that lived next door. Did you know she used to come by on Christmas Eve and stuff cookies into the mail slot in the front door? The things would fall apart before they ever hit the floor but it was the sweetest thing. She's the sweetest thing.

Well, maybe she should have this house then. I know she should and I'm going to keep helping her to get it. I got nowhere else to go right now anyway. I said I would wait right here for you and I will, no matter how long it takes.

No matter how long it takes.

Chapter 4

Blake and Mallory were sitting in a little neighborhood diner a few blocks away from the house. They were sipping strong and hot coffee, and applying their attention to giant plates filled with fluffy scrambled eggs, potatoes, toast and pancakes.

"Have you ever noticed that breakfast in a diner consists of starch, sugar and grease?" Mallory asked as she forked up a giant mouthful of syrup-dripping pancake and placed it in her mouth.

"That's why I enjoy it so much. I mean, don't get me wrong, it's not like I'm one of those guys that lives on potato chips and beer or anything like that. I do try to take care of myself sometimes."

"Well, you look like you take care of yourself." Mallory blushed as soon as the words left her mouth. She was not trying to date the man; she was trying to buy a house out from under his very attractive ass. Why was she always thinking about his bum?

Blake changed the subject. "So it seems as if one of our potential problems is gone. Then again, the historical society might decide that ghost would raise the value of that house."

Mallory met Blake's gaze over the rim of her coffee cup and she took a long sip before she asked, "Are you working with Lonnie to raise the price of the house?"

"Okay, let's just get this out in the open now, okay. Lonnie is my cousin but we don't know each other. We never met each other until recently, when Shannon Lewis died and I found out the house was empty and about to be sold.

"I know there are a lot of rumors that she had a child, she did. There's no sense in dressing it up or trying to save the reputation of the dead at this point. Not that anybody in this day and age would really care about that kind of thing anyway. She was my grandmother, but I never met her.

"I used to come down here and drive by the house and I always, always wanted to go inside of it. I knew from the time I was about sixteen that I wanted to live in that house. It's not something I'm willing to give up."

"I'm not willing to give it up either." Mallory stuck her fork into her pile of pancakes and left it there. "I used to pretend, when I was little girl, that I lived there. I used to wonder what it was like inside, too, so I guess we have the same curiosity. I never expected it to look the way it looks though, wow, what a mess."

"If Lonnie really is trying to sell it to a developer neither one of us is going to wind up with it." Blake was stating the truth and they both knew it.

Mallory changed the subject unexpectedly. "I'm very sorry to hear that you lost your grandmother. I'm even sorrier to hear that you didn't know her. I don't think many people knew her, and I'm not going to pretend that I did because I didn't.

"She was always very much a recluse, she hardly ever even came outside unless it was to scream at the guy that cut her grass. She was always positive that he was going to run over her azalea bushes or knock down her clotheslines. It would've been funny, if it wasn't so sad."

"I still wish I'd met her. I don't know if Lonnie even knew her either."

Mallory said, "I can answer that for you. No. Shannon hated her aunt, and all her aunt's offspring. Lonnie is descended from that line somehow or another, I never really asked but anyway… My mom and dad used to laugh about it when I was little. They said that her aunt came by one day to try to talk some sense into her and managed to rile Ms. Lewis up to the point where she actually came out of the house, jumped into that old car of hers and she tried to run her aunt down right there in the driveway."

Blake burst into laughter. He had not expected to be able to hold a conversation with Mallory, much less one that was so easy and relaxed. It was almost as if they weren't fighting over the same thing, and he almost wished they weren't. Her hand was lying on the table, and he put his own down beside it—not really touching her but just letting the heat of her hands seep over into his. It was pleasant, and he looked up into her soft eyes and found her staring back at him.

"We could work together."

"What do you mean?"

"I mean if we pooled our money we could get the house and then…we could share it."

The offer had been impulsive, and he had no idea why he had made it really. It was pretty obvious that she was determined to have that house, and she had good reasons for it— her reasons were just as good as his own. Maybe exactly what they needed was an alliance.

"I'm still not sure what you mean." Mallory wasn't sure what he meant, how could they share the house?

Blake leaned forward. "I have my architect's degree, but what I really love to do is build things. But not new things, I like to take old things that have been damaged and broken, and restore them. This house is the perfect project for me because of that. It's also huge, and quite frankly if there's even a dollar added to the price point it'll break my budget.

"What we could do is share the house, by turning it into a duplex. There's plenty of room, we could divide it up right down the middle. What do you say?"

Mallory stared at him, in a way it made perfect sense and it would actually solve all her problems. She would only be responsible for fixing half the house, which meant that some of her budget would not be lost and she could use it for other things which she dearly needed, like furniture. Or an office for her new business. "How would we decide how to divide it?"

Blake said, "It would not be as difficult as it seems. Not really, the house was set up with the premise of two wings so if you simply split them apart and put a wall in between, it would sort of naturally divide into a duplex. We can even incorporate the staircase into the division of it because it goes up and into the landing so we could put the wall in the direct center of the staircase so that we both have stairs and one half of the landing."

"Okay, all that sounds great but there is one problem."

Blake asked, "What's that?"

"I can't afford a new kitchen."

He crowed, "I knew it! You loved those appliances, say it! Say you loved them. You don't have to beat around the bush, you can have them!"

Mallory retorted, "You loved them! You should keep them!"

"I can't afford the laser surgery my eyes would require after looking at them," Blake chortled.

They both burst into gales of laughter. "They look like someone tossed slime at a stove and refrigerator," Blake choked out and Mallory laughed even harder.

**

After Blake dropped her off at home Mallory began to gather up the things she would need while she went to talk to the man who ran the local ad agency and looked over his books. Her mind was not at all on the task on hand, instead it was stuck on Blake.

So he had never known his grandmother. How sad was that? She could understand exactly why he wanted the house and if things were different she would have walked away and let him have it but things were far too dire for her.

The only other prospect was living with her mother for the next year or two or renting another place. Paying rent would quickly deplete her savings. Living with her mother for too long would drive her insane.

Could they really turn the house into a duplex? Did she want that?

How could she live that close to Blake and not give into the temptation that was constantly rising up in her every time he got near her?

She doubted it, he was far too irresistible.

What was wrong with her exactly? She had just gotten out of a relationship that had gone seriously south, the last thing she needed was to get hung up on another guy, especially one like Blake.

One like Blake, what did she mean by that exactly? He was different than the guys she usually dated, yes, but was that really a bad thing? Jim had been exactly the kind of guy she dated and look how that had turned out.

That brought her to another thought. What had happened to all the hurt that she had felt over his leaving? It had somehow vanished, and she was not sure why or how. It was like it had just disappeared as soon as she had gotten back to Golden.

Or as soon as she met Blake.

Frustrated by that thought she finished dressing, applying a little more mascara to her lashes and a small squirt of light floral perfume to her flesh before heading out.

She had better things to think about than a good-looking man in tight jeans…

**

Blake had dated several women over the last few years but none of them had come anywhere close to inciting the feelings that Mallory had created within him in just a matter of days. She had somehow managed to reach right inside of him and put a finger on his heart.

That disturbed him greatly. It was impossible to fall in love at first sight, but it seemed that he had. How was that possible? Mallory was obviously not interested in him, and she had the look of someone who was keeping people at bay for a damn good reason.

He walked into the hardware store, trying to get his mind off her by pricing some materials but that idea fell flat as soon as he saw Lonnie standing in an aisle scoping out a rake. He looked up, saw Blake and grinned that sickly little grin of his before he said, "Hello there. How did it work out with Mallory?"

"What do you mean?" Blake had a feeling that he knew exactly what Lonnie was getting at but he chose to try to sidestep it in the hopes that Lonnie would get the hint. No such luck was happening, it seemed, because Lonnie said, "She's feisty, isn't she?"

"Define feisty."

Lonnie ignored Blake's glower. "I don't blame you for chasing her but keep in mind that she likes the kind of guy that wears glasses and reads books."

"You say that like it's a bad thing too."

"I guess it is a bad thing, at least for guys like us. She doesn't seem to like them virile."

That Lonnie could even apply that word to himself was mind-boggling. Blake said, "Well that's her option, isn't it?"

"I guess it is, you would figure after she got dumped just a couple of days before she was supposed to walk down the aisle with that guy she was with up there in Chicago, she would change her mind."

"I'm sorry?"

"Oh come on, everyone in town's talking about it. She lost her job and fiancé all at once. She came home too, she had nowhere else to go, I hear the only money she's even got these days is the money she got back from her wedding. Serves her right if you ask me, she was always talking about how she couldn't wait to get out of here. Well, she sure enough had to come back didn't she, just goes to show she could not make it up there."

Blake punched him. It was a reflex action and one he was not sorry about. It wasn't even a hard punch, it was almost a tap but it knocked Lonnie straight off his feet and onto his ass in the middle of the floor.

Lonnie cried, "What did you do that for?"

"I'm sorry, my hands slipped as I was reaching for that rake behind you."

A snigger from the clerk put Lonnie back on his feet, his eyes narrowing down to mere slits as he said, "You're never going to get that house. I'll see to it that you won't! I would not sell it to you if you were the last person on earth!"

Blake walked out of the store. His thoughts were flying in all different directions and he really wished he had not run into Lonnie at all. Mallory had had a bad breakup that accounted for the sadness in her eyes and the way that she seemed to be so distant so much of the time. She just moved home, so that was a fresh wound.

The last thing on earth she needed was some guy like him messing around with her.

**

Mallory made it home that evening feeling discouraged and saddened. The day had not gone well, nothing had gone the way she had hoped and planned ever since she had come back to Golden and she was beginning to question the wisdom of returning home.

Maybe she should have just stayed gone; maybe she should have taken her chances in Chicago and hoped for the best, anything might have been better than this.

Her mom met her at the door, a slightly goofy grin on her face and a glass of wine in her hand. "There you are, dear! Come on in, we have been waiting for you!"

"We? Who's we, Mom?"

"Your friend Blake and me of course."

Her friend Blake? Mallory stared past her mother at Blake, who looked ridiculously at ease on her mother's overstuffed sofa. He gave her a sheepish grin and she tilted her head, trying to figure out what angle he was working. She had already agreed to try to work with him to obtain Gray Oaks so what else did he want?

"I made a giant roast," Cara announced, "and cobbler."

Of course she had. It was the same meal she made for every guy that she approved of—that was her silent but visible seal and stamp. Mallory gritted her teeth and waited until her mother left the room to hiss, "What are you doing here?"

"I don't know really. She saw me walking down the street…"

"Why were you walking down the street?"

"I like to walk down the street."

"Are you stalking me?"

"If I were stalking you I would not be walking down the street in plain sight. I certainly would not stop to talk to your mom and let her invite me to dinner. What kind of stalker does that?"

"A very good one!"

"Okay now, that is just a little rude, I think. Actually I'm not sure. Are you complimenting my stalking skills or accusing me of having them in the first place?"

"You are the most impossible man on the planet!"

His kiss cut off her words mid-sentence. It took her by surprise but it was a welcome surprise. She melted into him, unable to help herself from doing so. She could smell his cologne and his shampoo; see the tiny little mole on his neck and feel the slightly rough fabric of his shirt below her fingertips.

As kisses went it beat any kiss Jim had ever given her hands-down. It was a dangerous kiss, the kind of kiss that could make a woman forget what it was she had to lose, and how much it would hurt to be left by a man like this one.

When it ended she immediately wanted him to kiss her again but he took a long step away from her and said, "I just had to know if your lips were as sweet as they look. They are."

They were interrupted by Cara coming back in the room and announcing that dinner was ready. Mallory had gone silent, stricken mute by the power of the kiss and his presence in her home. There was so much more to this man than his slick surface suggested and she knew it, but how did she get past all the walls he had put up all around himself? Why did she even want to break past those walls?

Blake was impressed with Mallory's home and her mother and not just because it was obvious that both were extremely well cared for. The house was the low-slung little Cape Cod style cottage he had noticed the day before. He had always liked the place; it had always seemed so charming.

Cara was charming too and she was also a good cook. The roast was perfect: juicy and tender. The vegetables were firm but done to a turn and the bread was fresh, slathered in butter and homemade.

The table was set with pretty willow-patterned plates and the wine was excellent—a deep dark merlot that went down perfectly with the meal. Mallory was just picking at her food and he knew that was his fault. He had meant to leave her alone, to just stop things before they even got started because it was very clear that she did not need more heartache in her life, and yet he had shown up here anyway.

How could he have been so insensitive? He should have known better and he did actually. She had accused him of being a stalker and while that was not necessarily true he could and should have told her mother no when she asked him to join her for a glass of wine and some conversation.

The evening was enjoyable but tense. When he finally got up to take his leave Mallory walked him to the door and he wondered if she was doing that to make sure he really left. On the front porch they paused. The night pressed down and the moon had come out as well as the stars. The silvery light outlined her pale face and the vibrant flame of her hair. The soft curve of her cheek made him want to kiss her again, and nuzzle his face into the long creamy column of her neck.

"I should not have come here and bothered you like this."

"It's okay. I just don't think kissing you again is the best idea, especially if we are going to be neighbors."

"So you decided to give the duplex idea a try?"

Had she? It seemed she had. Mallory crossed her arms over her chest so he could not see the hardening ridge of her nipples below her shirt. How could he confuse her and turn her on so much all at the same time? She wanted him to kiss her again, even though she was saying she didn't.

Mallory was not used to playing games and she didn't like the feeling that she was playing one. She had always believed that honesty was the best policy but here she was, lying her butt off. She honestly thought him kissing her again was a splendid idea.

"I suppose so."

Blake said, "I guess we are in cahoots now, huh?"

She wanted to be in more than just cahoots with him. "Yes."

"Good night, Mallory. Thanks again for the great meal."

"Oh, it was not me, it was my mom."

"Tell her thanks again for me, please."

"I will." He walked off and she stood on the porch watching him go. His jeans outlined his bottom, the denim swaddling those firm ripe globes and her hands itched to touch him, to feel those muscular halves under her fingers.

"My God, that man has a walk the devil would envy. A butt the devil would envy too. What is wrong with you?"

"Nothing, Mom." She pushed her body away from the porch railing.

"Then why aren't you running after him?"

"Because I just got out of a relationship, I don't need another one."

Cara stopped her before she could walk into the house. "I never liked Jim. I guess I never bothered to hide that fact either."

"No, you didn't."

"Do you know why I never liked him?"

"No, why didn't you?"

"Because he was never in the same relationship that you were in, he was in something totally different."

Mallory turned away, her eyes glinting with tears. "Mom, I don't want to talk about this."

"I think you better do something before you end up as alone and sad as Shannon Lewis did. At least she had a romantic backstory to season her tragedy, all you have is your heart broken by a guy who never loved you as much as you loved him."

"I'll try to keep that in mind, Mom. Good night."

"I still think you should run after him and grab on tight."

"Stop reading romance novels, Mom, they are giving you a weird outlook on life."

"It's called hope, darling, you should try it sometime."

"No thanks. That is one brand of hope I just can't afford."

She meant that last bit. She also swore that she would never kiss Blake again, no matter how tempting it was.

Blake was telling himself the same thing. The last thing he needed to do was get involved with a woman who was clearly not interested in being involved with him.

He was going to leave her alone, no more walking past the house trying to get a glimpse of her. Okay, he had done that and yes, that was actually stalking—maybe not in a creepy trying to look into her windows or steal her panties kind of way but yes, it was stalking.

He had really not meant to intrude upon her life. Her mother's invitation had surprised him. What had surprised him even more was her mother's candid confession that she thought that perhaps the divorce between herself and Mallory's father, so late in their lives together, had created some serious trust issues within Mallory.

That and being dumped by the jackass ex that had apparently been planning his exit for quite some time. How could a man leave her like that? If that had been him he never would have walked away.

The motel loomed ahead. He stared at the unlovely building, seeing how it sagged in the weed-choked lot, its cinderblock sides glowing dimly under the sodium vapor lights. The roof was a bright red tile, put on during some burst of better times.

The windows were all covered with the heavy drapes that promised privacy but could not quite mask the sounds of the highway just beyond, and the cars and trucks parked in front of the rooms were all older, dingy and worn out.

The whole thing made him tired. He wanted to be at Gray Oaks, sitting out on the porch in a low-slung wicker sofa with his arm around Mallory's shoulder and the crickets whirring in the grass, the frogs croaking from the small pond that sat near the side yard of the property and the night birds singing from the branches of the towering live oak trees.

He went into his room, stripped and showered and then lay down on his bed. He closed his eyes, trying to banish the very tempting images that had been conjured up seemingly from thin air.

**

Mallory also lay in her bed, but like Blake she was not sleeping. She was thinking about Blake and she was also thinking about Jim. She knew it was not fair to compare the two. Jim was a cerebral man, one who believed that the mind was basically everything. He had eschewed physical labor, and in fact often exhibited an abhorrence of it that often bothered her.

Jim was content in his position in his life. Or at least he seemed to be, all up until that day she walked in to find him sitting there in his almost feminine little pose waiting for her to come home so that he could break the news to her that he was leaving.

She threw a pillow at the wall. She expected to feel sad, remembering that little scene but instead all she felt was angry. How dare he do that to her? She closed her eyes and it all came flooding back. She could see him sitting there, his light blue and heavily starched oxford shirt buttoned absolutely correctly and tucked in tightly around his lean waist. A waist that stayed lean due to his constant, strict dieting and often even stricter juicing and fasting programs.

He had had his fingers laced together and placed carefully around one knee. The ankle of the foot on top had been placed precisely between his ankle and the knee of the other leg. The creases on his slacks had been sharp enough to cut butter and his high cheekbone face had worn an appropriately solemn expression.

How long had he worked to get his face into just that expression? Had he practiced in front of the mirror just to get it right? She wouldn't doubt it since Jim had done more strange things than that over the course of the time they had been together.

She sat up, her eyes taking in the familiar lines and spaces of her childhood bedroom. The full bed sat in one corner, across from the windows that looked out onto the side yard of Gray Oaks. The tall white dresser that matched her headboard and footboards had held her clothes since she was twelve. The fluffy blue-and-white rug on the floor had been laid that same year as well.

The year she had been twelve, that had been a big year for her. Her outgrown bedroom furniture had vanished to make way for a larger bed and dresser, and the vanity table with a mirror so that she could start to apply the makeup that she coveted so much back then. She also had begun to hang up posters of movie stars on the wall. Most of those posters were down now, replaced by prints of Picasso's works as well as prints from other artists that she had admired throughout the years.

The curtains on the window had been hand-sewn by her grandmother. The comforter on her bed had a stain from the night she had hosted a slumber party and one of the girls had carelessly spilled hot cocoa on the bed.

Everything about the room was so familiar, and so welcoming. She found herself comparing it to the bedroom she had had in Chicago, not the one she had as a single woman but the one she had shared with Jim. It had been perfect, that bedroom. It had had the perfect furniture, the perfect carpet and even the perfect couple in it and yet it had not been perfect at all, not really.

She still had the furniture. A king-size sleigh bed whose rock maple gleamed thanks to years of lemon and beeswax being rubbed into it, a matching nightstand, dresser and chest of drawers with a large mirror. It occurred to her that Jim had never paid a dime for that furniture. He had gone along with her when she had gone to pick the furniture out, both of them having decided that her small convertible bed and his only slightly larger full bed were no longer sufficient since they were moving in together.

He had insisted on that very set, and she had never questioned whether or not she even liked it. Lying there now, in the bed that she had slept in for most of her youth, she found herself questioning if she actually did like it. Why had she had the moving company bring it all the way to Golden?

It was sitting in a storage unit, along with most of her other things, waiting for the day when she would have her own place again. But when she did get her own place again did she really want that furniture in there?

Blake… Now there was a man who believed in doing things that were physical. She could not imagine him picking out a bed at all. She could imagine him saying something like, "Whatever you think works well enough." But was that any better?

Maybe she was being entirely unfair. Blake was a very sensitive guy for all his masculine virility. Just thinking of his masculinity made her blush. When he had been kissing her she had felt just how hard and eager he was, she had known that she had excited him as much as he excited her and in a way that was very gratifying but it was also terrifying.

Jim had never been much of a lover. In fact he had often treated sex as if it were perfunctory duty that he participated in only because he had no choice.

Maybe her mother was right. Maybe Jim had never been in the same relationship she was in.

Blake… Now there was a man who would be all in. He would hold nothing back. He would not know how to hold back unless you gave him a manual and explained it to him.

The thin silver light of the moon filtered down into her window, through the open curtains, and Mallory slowly got up and went to the window, leaning far out of it and looking over at Gray Oaks. The slight tower that rose from the second floor of to the third on the same side of the house that her bedroom overlooked was also touched by the moonlight.

Mallory frowned, sure she was hallucinating. For a moment—a brief and quickly gone moment—it seemed as if there were a figure standing in that window looking back at her. Mallory had seen Shannon Lewis all her young life, from a distance at any rate. Shannon had always seemed old, frail and bent. Whoever had been looking out at her from that window had been young, with shining black hair that cascaded to the middle of the back of her slim figure clad in a thin nightgown.

The moonlight continued to beam down, outlining the crisp little blades of grass, the delicate petals of the lilies that grew rampant and the blooming roses on the bushes. Those flowers sent out their heavenly scents and she leaned further out the window, closing her eyes as she inhaled them. How could anyone stand to sell something so beautiful just to turn it into another soulless and featureless apartment building?

Well, it wasn't going to happen if she could help it.

What a sweet girl. I'm glad she made it back from wherever it was she went to because her mama was very lonely without her. Her mama used to think that I didn't see her watching me, but of course I did. It was a shame when her husband left her but I could've told her that was going to happen years before it did, not that she did not know it herself. The two of them were staying together for that girl and after she was gone they just stayed together because they were used to each other. They were rubbing along like two old horses in a harness.

I know a lot of people thought I was crazy, that I should've moved on after George died. Plenty of people told me so too. That's because they had the kind of love that happens from the outside not the kind of love that grows from the inside.

You should really hurry, George, I know you're still out there somewhere, trying to get back. I know it's been hard for you and I tried a lot of times to make it easier for you but dying the way you did made it easy for you to get lost.

It's such a very long way home, isn't it? Oh well, at least that girl over there made it back all in one piece even though she might think she lost some parts of herself along the way.

Chapter 5

A week went by. Louise informed Blake and Mallory both that Lonnie had indeed gotten a developer on the hook. She was as unhappy about it as they were because if the developer bought she would be cut right out of her hefty commission.

The news she gave them a few days after that was equally depressing. The developer had offered a price that was far beyond anything the two of them could hope to match even if they did pool their resources.

Blake drove over to the house, and on an impulse he went to Mallory's front door and knocked. She opened the door and he couldn't help but be stunned all over again by her beauty. That day she was wearing a pair of plain denim shorts with a white T-shirt and her hair was pulled up in a simple ponytail, though little wisps and curls had escaped it to fall around her face. She looked young and innocent and heartbreakingly lovely.

Almost before he knew what he was going to say he blurted out, "I don't suppose we could go over there and set up the place to booby-trap the developer."

For the first time in almost a week Mallory laughed. "Are you serious?"

"I can't think of anything else to do, can you?"

"Well, no, not really. I don't suppose you could actually give the developer the phone number for the historical society and let those women talk to him. They could talk him out of anything, I bet."

"It's too bad we simply can't ask my grandmother to make an appearance when the developer shows up. Maybe she could scare him out of wanting to buy the place."

He was standing so close to her, his firm yet soft lips near enough to touch if she would only move just a slight bit closer herself. Don't do it, don't do it, she told herself but her body wasn't listening to her brain. She moved a little bit closer, so close that he could smell her sweet perfume and see the small dab of jelly on one corner of her mouth from the toast she had been eating for breakfast.

The kiss was natural, unplanned and intense but sweet. Their mouths met, clung to each other's and his arms wrapped around her, pulling her tighter to his embrace. Both of them needed this; it was foolish but they couldn't stop it.

When they finally did break apart the only thing he could manage to utter was, "Wow."

Blake began to laugh. "I hope that's a compliment."

"Oh it is, it is. In fact I think you should do that again."

"I think you're right."

He did kiss her again, slowly and softly but meaningfully. Long moments passed while they stood there on her front porch just kissing each other and reveling in the nearness of the other.

Finally they broke apart again, both of them wearing slightly dazed expressions. Mallory asked, "You want to sit down?"

"Maybe I should."

"How about some tea? I just made a fresh pitcher."

"I would love some. You didn't get converted to unsweet tea while you were up there in the North, did you?"

Mallory laughed at that. "No. In fact it was this huge bone of contention between me and my ex. He hated sweet tea, he thought it was disgusting and you know I grew up on it so I love it."

She turned and went back into the house to fetch the tea, and before the screen door swung shut he saw how her pert little rump swung from side to side as she walked. That was the last thing on earth he needed today, she was going to give him a heart attack right here on her porch!

When she came back out she set out a pitcher and two glasses choked with ice and lemon on a little table in front of the small patio set sitting on the porch. "So it looks like neither one of us is going to get the house."

"It looks that way."

She poured the tea and handed him a glass. Blake looked down into it, wishing there was something he could say but not knowing what to say. Finally he just said, "I'm sorry you came all the way home and didn't get what you came here for."

Mallory laughed. "Who told you that I came here just to get the house?"

Blake said, "Nobody. I just assumed that that's what you came for." There was no way in hell he was going to tell her what Lonnie had said.

Mallory eased that awkwardness by saying, "I moved back home because I had to. The company I worked for in Chicago downsized and there's a huge unemployment rate there right now. You know, it's the weirdest thing, when I was growing up here all I could think about was how important it would be to leave here and to be somebody out there in the bigger world but the whole time I was gone from here, I missed it.

"I came back and I honestly thought that it was the end of the world. That I had failed somehow but do you know, I don't think that's true. I started my own little business and while I will never make the kind of money I was making in Chicago I also don't have the kind of expenses that I had there. And I won't miss home anymore, because I am home.

"And also, before somebody else tells you, you should know that I was engaged to be married. I had a whole fund set up for a house and everything but he left right before the invitations went out. It seems that he found me unfit to be a wife."

"I just can't imagine how that's possible. I mean, how could anyone leave you?"

"I'm a really bad cook."

The laughter that filled the air between them was real. Blake said, "Did he not know how to navigate his way to the nearest McDonald's?"

Mallory said, "Oh, Jim would never eat McDonald's. It wasn't even in his vocabulary."

Blake feigned horror. "He wouldn't eat McDonald's? Why that's positively barbaric!"

"Actually, he thought eating fast food was barbaric."

"Do you miss him?"

She met his eyes squarely. "At first I thought it would die. I was so heartbroken and so upset but recently it occurred to me that it wasn't really him that I missed, it was everything else. It was being the successful accountant, the big fancy apartment in the extremely nice area of Chicago. It was being somebody's fiancée, and all of the things that came along with that.

"A few days ago it occurred to me that I wasn't crying because I missed him and I wasn't hurt because it was over, I was crying and hurt because of the way it ended. It was so childish the way he did things. He waited until the last minute instead of just being honest with me. If he wasn't sure like he said, if he didn't think I was suitable he should have said so in the first place instead of living with me all those years.

"I had to actually think about why he would've done that and the truth is—I'm an accountant. I did the math. He could never have afforded all the things that we had together on his own, I was a convenience for him. Now that I know all that I don't miss him at all."

Blake said, "If that's how he thought of you, he never deserved to have you in the first place."

Mallory said, "I'm beginning to see that. So, how about you? What did you do in Atlanta?"

Blake said, "Well, I told you, I'm an architect. I worked on a whole lot of restoration projects and that was really what interested me the most. There's just something about taking a house and making it new again, allowing its history to live on, that is just incredible and almost unbearably exciting."

Mallory asked, "Is that part of the reason why you want Gray Oaks so much? I mean I know you want it because Shannon was your grandmother, could it be that you're trying to restore a history and maybe make a little of your own with her in some way?"

She had hit the nail directly on the head. Blake would never have been able to put those thoughts and feelings into words like she just had and he said, "Yes. I think in a way having the house and being able to restore it would be like being able to get to know her, and by extension maybe my grandfather."

The two of them sat there in companionable silence not realizing that someone was watching over them.

Oh, oh my. George you should probably hurry up and get here! There's your grandson, sitting right next door! Well now I feel kind of bad about throwing the poor boy into the wardrobe... And how was I to know he was our grandchild? So he wants the house, and so does she. It's easy to see the two of them belong together.

So, that no good son of a gun Lonnie wants to sell this house off to a developer, huh? I know what developers do. I still had the television even if I didn't get out much. I watched that Lifetime channel a lot and they were always showing movies about some greedy developer coming into a small town and tearing it apart.

They could put a lot of things here, there's not a lot of the original land left but there's enough of it. It would destroy this whole house and everything that it stood for. They would tear down every moment of my family's memories and never know what they were destroying… Or care.

Okay then. Let Lonnie bring some developer into my home. If he thought those historical society women ran out in a hurry he hasn't seen anything yet! I will see to it that Mallory and Blake do not lose out on this house, because I think if they do then they will lose out on each other.

Oh I know, I know George. I meddle far too much. But I'm a lonely old lady living in a house that's been quiet for far too long. I know you can find your way back to me. I know it. But, in the meantime I might as well enjoy myself a little bit. What's the fun in being dead if you can't scare the hell out of a few folks sometimes?

"That must be the developer." Mallory gestured toward the car pulling into the driveway of the house next door. "That's quite a fancy rig he's driving."

Blake said, "Yes, it is. The car cost more than Lonnie's asking for the house."

"If there was ever a time I wish I had won the lottery…"

"I know, me too."

"I suppose we could always go toss on some sheets and run to the house screaming 'Get out while you still can or die!' at him."

"He's a developer, they have no fear. I hear they don't have a heart either."

"Even vampires have a heart, after all they have to have something to stab the stake into."

"Developers are different kind of vampire."

"Oh really? What kind of vampire would that be?"

"The kind that never dies, they just go to a new suburb and regroup."

Mallory said, "I wish I had known you a long time ago. You are probably the most amusing man on the planet."

"Oh, and here I thought you were keeping me around for my good looks."

"You aren't lacking in looks either." She looked down in her glass. "Listen, I don't want to get caught up in something that is bound to end. If you don't get the house you won't be staying, I take it."

"Who said that? I can keep on living at the Peek-a Loo."

Mallory almost choked. "You're staying there? My God, don't you know that that is the motel of sin? Every cheating man in town knows the desk clerk by name and the women who show up are always somebody else's."

"I think I heard that. That might explain the gunfire I heard last night right below my window."

She sputtered laughter. "Either you're a huge liar or that place has gotten worse over the years. Seriously, I don't think it really deserves its bad reputation, it's just rundown and a little ragged around the edges.

"Either way, nobody deserves to have to live there. What would you do if you're in town?"

"There's a few places looking for a good restoration man."

Mallory tilted her chin toward the man walking up to the house next door. "Maybe you could go to work for him since he seems to have plenty of money to spare."

Blake said, "I think I'd rather not, but thank you."

Later, they would sit around and talk about what happened next but they would never be able to describe it exactly.

Lonnie had just arrived, his rictus grin firmly in place and his bony hands practically rubbing together at the sight of the expensive foreign car sitting in the driveway. His pleasure did not last very long, and with good reason. The house did indeed pull inward. They could even hear it, there was a sudden inhalation that sounded like a giant monster was drawing breath, then there was a loud cracking sound, almost thunderous in the air.

Every one of Gray Oaks's windows and doors began to slam open and shut. The windows banged and rattled almost musically, the sashes hitting the seals so hard that it looked as if the glass would shatter at any moment. The front door squeaked and groaned but it was flung back and forth anyway.

If that was not enough the boards on the porch began to sway up and down, almost as if there was a body of water beneath them causing a tidal wave, but one created of wood and cement rather than water.

From somewhere inside the old house came the sound of screaming, and while Mallory and Blake were both certain that some of the screaming was coming from the developer there were other voices screaming as well: men, women and even children. It sounded like an entire cacophony had been loosed inside those walls.

Lonnie stood on the shaking walkway, his face going pale and his hands coming up in front of his body in a burst of involuntary applause or prayer, from where she sat Mallory could not say which one it was. It was easy to see that he wanted to turn tail and run and also equally easy to see that he was still hoping to make that sale.

Any hopes he'd had of selling to that developer were dashed, however. The house stopped shaking, the noises stopped and the front door flew open. The well-dressed developer was hurtled out the door as if something had picked him up and tossed him along like a basketball. He skidded along the overgrown front lawn on the backside of his tailored slacks. His overly polished Italian loafers gleamed in the sunlight and when he finally did fetch up, half in and half out of a flower bed, he had obviously decided that Gray Oaks was not the house for him.

Mallory and Blake wasted no time. Without even thinking about it they both jumped to their feet and ran. They got to the walkway just as the developer made it to his feet and stood there, dusting off the back of his pants and glaring at Lonnie. "Maybe you could give me a small glimpse into what it was that you were thinking when you invited me out here to see this disaster of a place. I have just been assaulted by someone, or something and I refuse to deal with that type of thing."

"Oh, Lonnie just doesn't think much," Mallory put in cheerfully. "He didn't bother telling you the house was haunted, did he?"

The developer gave her an equally icy glower. "And who might you be?"

"She just wants to buy the house!" Lonnie's voice was high-pitched and his face was red. His overly large Adam's apple bobbed up and down his skinny throat as he said, "This is probably something the two of them cooked up together to keep you from buying the house! They want it, and they're ticked off because I wouldn't sell it to them."

"Oh, don't be ridiculous, Lonnie." Blake gave the developer a hard and level look. "You're welcome to buy the house, but maybe before you do you should talk to the women who run the historical society. They were out here the other day and I think they had a slightly odd experience themselves."

Lonnie said, "Even if it is haunted, who cares? That just makes it more exciting! It gives the place character! And character is what it's all about these days with real estate! Anyone can go rent an average apartment or an average home but this is renting an experience! Think of the publicity it will get you, developer builds on site of haunted house!"

The developer said, "I can't sell that as an experience. Maybe one or two apartments would rent to those weirdos that like ghosts gallivanting around the place but the majority of people want to be left alone and live in peace. What just happened to me in there was similar to being violated. I cannot imagine my tenants would appreciate that, and if word got out that it was happening I would be stuck with a lot of apartments that are just sitting empty, which means they would just be sucking money out of my pocket."

Blake's eyebrows nearly hit his hairline. "Violated? Sir, surely you're exaggerating. That ghost is quite friendly. The only thing she's ever done to me is toss me into a wardrobe."

Mallory chimed in, "Yes, and she let him right back out again!"

Lonnie gave them both a filthy stare. "Pay no attention to them, I told you they want the house. They probably rigged up a bunch of special effects in there so that nobody else would buy it."

"I tell you what, you spend the night in there and come back out and tell me that it's not haunted and I will buy the damn thing and what's more, I will double the price." The developer dusted his hands off as if the matter were closed as far as he was concerned. He did not expect Lonnie to take the dare and neither did Mallory, as Lonnie did not seem like the brave type.

But Lonnie said, "Did you say you would double the price?"

Damn! Lonnie would do anything for money. Mallory looked over at Blake who raised his eyebrows at her and she said, "He once ate worms to make five bucks."

Lonnie cried out in a peevish voice, "Oh come on, give me a break. I was in third grade!"

The developer shook his head. "If you spend the night in that house—if you're brave enough to spend the night in that house I will buy it, but otherwise the deal's off."

"Can I ask you how you are going to find out if he really stays in there?" Mallory asked. She knew Lonnie well, if there was a way he could weasel out of something he would find it. This was going to be fine, even if she did have to dress up and chase him all up and down the hallways of that house.

"I suppose we will have to webcam." The developer looked like he was a man with a sense of humor because he was smiling now and there was actually laughter lurking in his eyes. "Some things can't be faked and I don't think you could fake being in that house."

"No, I don't think you could." Mallory was trying hard not to laugh herself. "Look at it this way, Lonnie, if nothing happens, you will come out twice as rich as you wanted to be in the first place. If something does happen then you have video proof of it. You could sell the footage to some reality show and make a fortune that way."

Blake added, "It sounds like you don't have anything at all to lose there, buddy."

And just like that—they talked Lonnie into spending the night at Gray Oaks.

**

As it turned out the developer, whose name was Greg, did have a sense of humor. When Lonnie declared that it would be unfair for Blake and Mallory to be able to "sneak in and out of the house and trick him" while he was trying to spend the night there, Greg agreed. He then suggested that all three of them could watch Lonnie's movements through the house from the living room of his own home.

Mallory and Blake agreed, mostly just because they didn't want to give Lonnie a fighting chance to pretend that they were behind the haunting of the house. As they were following Greg to his house Blake asked, "Mallory, do you believe the house is haunted?"

"I didn't used to. I mean, I lived next door to it my entire life and I never saw anything happen. I heard a whole lot of people say that it was haunted but... I mean I never saw anything, not even a light in the window that would say that it was."

"Okay, are we going to pretend that that whole wardrobe thing didn't really happen?"

"No, it happened. I was just afraid to say anything about it because I thought you might think I was crazy."

"I have to admit, it was a very scary feeling sliding along that floor."

"It looked pretty scary. You must have been flying along at around fifteen or so miles an hour. I wanted to help you but I didn't know how."

"If it happens again, why don't you grab ahold of my legs and either try to stop me or go along for the ride with me?" He asked that question with that same devilish little grin that always made her heart flutter just a little more than she would've liked it to.

Mallory began to laugh, she just couldn't help herself. "Blake, if the house really is haunted and Greg doesn't buy it, could we make this work? Could we really divide the house?"

"I could think of a few alternatives."

Mallory's heart gave a little squeeze. She could think of a few alternatives, too, like love and marriage. Children: a whole new generation being raised within the walls of that giant Victorian home.

She was pretty sure that that was not what he was thinking so she didn't say anything or ask him to expound upon the subject.

That was actually exactly what Blake meant. It was absolutely utterly crazy—he barely knew this woman but he was madly in love with her. He could see himself spending his entire life with her, right there in that house. He could see them having children, growing old together, caring for each other and remodeling and renovating the house together. He could see them enjoying it and each other for the rest of their lives.

He was afraid to say that out loud. If he did she would probably grab for the door handle and toss herself out into the street. He probably didn't have enough horsepower under his engine to catch up with her, either, if she took a notion to run.

Greg lived in a completely modern slab of granite and glass. Blake and Mallory exchanged looks that said very clearly what they thought of the place although they never said it out loud. The inside of Greg's place was just as sleek, modern and unappealing to them, although it was obvious that he took a great deal of pride in it. He took them into a room that featured a giant pool table, a large-screen TV, comfortable recliners and a lot of other masculine-type goodies. Since the sun was about to set, Lonnie was due at the house. Greg hooked his laptop up to his TV somehow so that they could watch it on the larger screen and they all sat down to see what would happen.

Lonnie did arrive, and it was obvious from the way that he was talking into the small portable camera that Greg had given him that he was incredibly nervous and trying to pretend that he wasn't.

He made his way up to the porch and stood there, his hand reaching towards the doorknob and the keys dangling from his fingers. His Adam's apple bobbed up and down once more before he finally got up the courage to insert the key in the lock and press the door open.

Lonnie switched on the lights and Mallory leaned forward, her eyes riveted to the screen. Beside her Blake and Greg did the same. Lonnie said, in a quavering half-whisper, "See, nothing to it."

He stood in the foyer, looking right to left as if trying to decide which way to go. Finally he said, "I think I've checked out the living room. The upstairs is pretty hot."

"No crap," Blake said. "There's no air-conditioning up there but yet he wants someone to pay an outrageous amount of money for that house."

"That's called business," Greg said comfortably. "Although I have to say I would never buy a house without air-conditioning, that would really be uncomfortable."

Mallory hushed them. Lonnie was walking into the living room now and it was obvious by the way that the camera was jerking up and down that he was either nervous and shaking or he was trying to record everything in case there really was a ghost he could make a buck off hiding somewhere around the corner.

Mallory was nervous and tense. Blake's hand lay on the couch beside hers and she looked down at it, before she nudged her pinky slightly towards his. For a moment their fingers just sort of almost met and then he moved his hand over and enveloped hers with his own.

He turned his head and smiled at her and she smiled back. All of her anxiety melted away. So what if she didn't get this house? Did it really matter? What did matter was that she had found something even better than a house, she had found Blake.

Lonnie sat himself down on the couch and looked around. He spun the camera around his head and down the floor towards his feet. He was getting into it now, pretending he was the narrator of some reality show or something, and Mallory wanted to reach right through the television screen and give him a good hard shaking.

Where was the ghost? Where was Shannon? If there was ever a time for her to show up, now was it. As if to prove that point Lonnie said, "Looks like I'm going to get double for this ratty old place after all. I told you there was no such thing as ghosts."

The words had barely left his mouth before he was yanked up off the sofa and dangled from the ceiling by an invisible hand. His screams echoed and Greg jumped to his feet, his mouth hanging open as he stuttered out, "That is just what happened to me! Do you see that?"

Mallory did see it. The look on Blake's face told her he saw it too and that he was equally astonished. Lonnie was screaming like a banshee. Most of what he was yelling had something to do with the fact that he wanted out of that house and never wanted to see it again.

Mallory said, "Well, I guess he can't say we're behind this one."

Blake said, "Wow, look at him go!"

Lonnie was spinning around the living room now, his feet not touching the floor. It didn't look like he was in pain but it was very apparent that he was scared witless. His screams were high-pitched enough to shatter glass and Mallory put her hands to her ears, wincing as one particularly loud and strident shout echoed through the camera and into the television. Greg grabbed the remote and turned the volume down.

Mallory asked, "Should we go get him?" Blake and Greg looked at each other and just shrugged. Mallory rolled her eyes. Guys, they would sit here all night long watching poor Lonnie get dragged across that floor like a puppet whose strings had got lost somewhere and never make a move to help him simply because they thought the whole thing was funny.

Okay, it was funny. She did not particularly like Lonnie but she still felt a little sorry for him though.

Lonnie yelled, "I won't sell it to the developer! Will that make you happy, Grandma Lewis?"

Immediately his grotesque parody of a dance stopped. The lights blinked off then on again and Lonnie looked around like a frightened little child who had just been caught stealing. "Now come on, Grandma Lewis, you know I own this house fair and square."

He was snatched back up in the air and this time he was dangled by his foot from somewhere around the center of the light socket. When he stopped screaming he was set down as neatly and gently on the sofa as if he had never been lifted off it.

"Still want the house?"

Greg looked over at Blake and said, "I can't sell that. I could never turn it into apartments and renovating it just to sell it as a single house makes no sense from a financial perspective. If I can't make money off it, the house has no value to me."

Mallory did a happy little dance. Things were not really solved, but they were better than they had been. In the house Lonnie shouted out, "Hey, y'all come get me!"

Chapter 6

Lonnie was gone and Mallory and Blake were standing in front of the house. Mallory's mother came out on the porch, saw them standing there and gave them a little wave of her hand before going back inside.

"Your mother seems nice," Blake observed.

"She's a big romance reader. She's probably hoping you have a horse stuck somewhere in your back pocket. That way you could just ride off into the sunset with me, all your armor clanking as we go."

"I don't have a horse or armor, but I do have a lot of other things."

Mallory turned to face him, suddenly shy. She looked up in his eyes and said, "What are we doing?"

Blake said, "I do believe it's called falling in love."

"I thought it was losing my mind."

"I hear the two have a lot in common."

"Blake, we hardly know each other. What if this is just some crazy infatuation that wears off?"

"How will we know if we don't try?"

The man had a point. Mallory looked back at the house and as she stared at the window of the bedroom that had belonged to Shannon Lewis she saw a tiny slender flame flare up.

"Do you know she never gave up on him? Until the day she died she waited for him to come back to her. My mom said that when she was a little girl people still talked about all the séances and stuff she used to hold in the hopes of bringing his spirit to her."

Blake put his arm around her neck and pulled her close to him. She was just tall enough that her head came exactly to his chin and she filled up all of the spaces left by the curves and turns of his own body. It was as if she had been made to be beside him, she fit there so perfectly and he knew she felt the same but was afraid to say so.

"Did you know they met at a bus stop and from the moment they met until the moment he was shipped out to fight, they were almost always together? Even when he was supposed to be on base, locked down, he snuck out and went to her. He could have been court-martialed or labeled a deserter. It was a hell of a risk but he had to take it, he could not leave her alone. He slept right beside her in her bedroom at Gray Oaks."

Mallory had not known that and she stared at him, saying, "You know about all of that? I thought nobody knew. He was here, at Gray Oaks? I don't think anyone knew about that."

"My dad's parents knew all about it. When I was about fifteen my grandmother was dying and she told me about it. She said it didn't matter anymore—that everyone who could have been hurt by the truth was either dead or too old to care."

Mallory could not contain her curiosity. "How did they meet?"

"George, my grandfather, was riding in a car with some friends of his when he saw Shannon, who had just gotten off the bus at her stop, walking along the sidewalk and eating an ice cream cone. One of his friends whistled at her and she flipped him the bird, something girls just did not do in those days. It tickled George to no end so he made his friend stop the car and he got out and he walked beside her all the way to her house. When they got here he went inside and told her parents that he was going to marry her."

Tears rose up in Mallory's eyes. "They didn't know each other but he wanted to marry her, they fell in love at first sight. How did they do that when love at first sight does not even exist?"

"Oh, yes it does. They are proof of that. Love at first sight is incredibly real. They were with each other almost every day. They poured their hearts out to each other and they got to know each other without all the things that usually get in the way.

"George had already shipped out when Shannon found out she was pregnant but she thought he would come home and she could keep my father. It was all they talked about in their letters, raising him here at Gray Oaks."

"How do you know that?" Mallory asked.

"My grandmother got the letters that she sent to my grandfather from the War Department. They were with his body and they got shipped back with his body after he died. I read those letters, and I know my grandfather really wanted to come home and to be with her. His parents were not exactly keen on the idea and when he died they got together with her parents and they all decided that it was the best thing, giving my father to them."

The tears ran down Mallory's face. "She spent her whole life in that house waiting for George to come back to her, and she had to know that he never would."

"Maybe he will one day. Maybe, maybe he just got lost. Maybe he's trying to find his way back."

Mallory said, "Wouldn't it be wonderful if he did find his way back, if he could come back to her?"

Blake said, "Yes, it would."

The candle in the window blew out. The crickets sang in the grass and the leaves on the old oak trees whispered as they rubbed together in the slight breeze. The smell of magnolia and honeysuckle lay over everything. From somewhere in the distance they heard a child laughing and they could smell the faint scent of somebody's dinner cooking from one of the other houses.

"This was the best place to grow up."

Blake looked askance at her. "You mean at your house or on the street?"

"On the street, in this neighborhood. The funny thing is, I never realized how much of a part of this neighborhood she was until now, and now she's gone."

Blake said, "Somehow I tend to doubt that she's really gone. She did say she would never leave this house until George came to fetch her."

"I wish there was a way we could help him get home, get back to her."

"Mallory, I know it's soon and I know we don't really know each other. It's like history is repeating itself all over again and this time we have a chance to do it right. I want that house, you want that house and I think only a fool would not know that we want each other.

"We could try it. We could work on the house together and if we hate it or each other we could agree to not do it."

Mallory took a deep breath and looked at the house and then look back at Blake. "I think we could try."

**

The sound of saws filled the air and Mallory dodged a man carrying out a huge basket of trash. The house was coming along, but in the beginning stages of restoration it looked like the house was in worse shape than ever.

It was a little discouraging, in truth. Mallory was slogging through a kitchen stripped of the terrible appliances and the bare sections of wall were showing signs of warp and rot. Repairing that was going to cost more than they had imagined. The floors had dark stains and discolorations and the windows needed replacing; at some point Shannon had boarded them over and then took the boards down again, leaving nail holes and small cracks in the sashes and glass.

The cabinets were in sad shape, they were almost separating from the wall. They showed signs of mold along the edges. The dishes that had been in them had all been good china but quite a lot of it had been broken and cracked beyond repair. The pieces that had been good had been washed and were awaiting new cabinets to go into. Someone had suggested that they sell the pieces so that they could get money to make more repairs but neither of them had been interested in doing that.

Mallory opened a closet, expecting to find a hoard of canned foods or something like that but instead she found something far better: a stack of paintings. Not just any paintings either—paintings that had Shannon's name on the bottom.

Thumbing through them, Mallory realized two things immediately: Blake had been wrong in thinking that his grandmother had not ever seen his father…or him. She had, somehow, and she had painted them.

"Blake! Come here!"

He did and when he got into the kitchen she burst into laughter all over again. He was covered in plaster dust and sawdust, his hair was almost white from it and his eyes peered out of it like two blue searchlights.

"You're going to pay for that laugh," he warned her good-naturedly.

"Look what I found," Mallory crowed.

Blake looked through the paintings, his face going solemn as his fingers followed the brush strokes. "My grandparents lied to me."

"I don't think they did. These look like they were made from photographs, not from life. See, look here, here are some paintings that she did from life—that's my mom, see? That's me, as a little girl. I remember that day—it was Easter and we were having a big neighborhood party in the backyard. She must have drawn the outlines that day and then painted it in later. But there's a difference in the paintings of you and your dad, they were done from photographs. The paintings are all of the two of you posed, never just hanging out or whatever. This looks like a school photo, like she painted you from a school photo.

"Maybe your grandparents actually sent pictures of you to her."

"Why would they do that?"

"Maybe she asked."

Blake just looked at the paintings. His grandparents were dead and had been for years, they were never going to be able to answer his questions about these paintings so this was going to remain a mystery. But it still made him feel better to know that his grandmother had known he was alive. The paintings of him stopped right around the time he turned six... Wait, that had been when his grandmother died!

Was it possible? Had his grandmother had the kind of mercy that only a woman would have for another woman who had lost her child? Had she snuck around and sent pictures to Shannon? He supposed it was possible, anything was after all.

It was a mystery, yes, but it was one whose solution was not important at all. What mattered was that his grandmother had known of his existence and had cared enough about him to paint his face, his little body. And his father's as well.

"Can we hang them once we get the walls finished?"

Mallory would ask that question. Her eyes were fastened on his in a sincere and hopeful gaze. It wasn't just that she thought these paintings should be hung up because they were of him and his father, she wanted these paintings hung up because she honestly liked the paintings. He knew she really appreciated art, she'd been dragging him into the local museums and craft shows in search of things for the house. He knew that she knew good art when she saw it.

"Of course we can. They should have been hung all those years. I'm guessing she didn't hang them because it was painful to look at them."

Mallory frowned. "Do you think she's going to mind us hanging them up?" Neither of them bothered trying to dismiss that question as silly. They both knew that Shannon was still there, still in the house and if she didn't like something, well…

Blake said, "I guess we'll know soon enough if she doesn't want them up, won't we?"

"Yes, we will."

Blake went back to work and so did Mallory. As she worked she allowed herself to think of what it was exactly that she was doing. She knew, as an accountant, that what she was doing was absolutely insane. She and Blake had agreed to keep the house as it was, not to divide it up at all. They had pooled their money and bought the house outright. Then they had begun doing the work, most of it themselves in order to keep costs down.

They both had gotten jobs as well: Mallory was doing the accounting work for several of the firms in town and Blake was working as an architect at a local firm whose specialty was building large, modern subdivisions (a job he actually hated but did because it paid him enough to afford the renovations on Gray Oaks). So they did the work on the house as they had time.

As a result summer had faded into fall and it was now edging into winter. They were hoping to have the house done completely by Christmas but they had run into a few obstacles along the way, including larger power bills than they expected and longer work hours on their regular jobs than they would've liked. On top of that, for an entire month they had been forced to stay at her mother's house because the hot water heater had not only gone out, most of the plumbing pipes had exploded right along with it.

After Mallory and Blake had both earned a fairly large bonus at their respective jobs, which they had also pooled together, they found themselves in the enviable position of being able to hire a few people to come in and help them. The work was moving a lot faster now, for which they were both grateful. Even though the house did look like it was a wreck they both knew that it would soon be put back together and better than ever.

Because they were forced to be together, to deal with a high amount of stress and to do without a lot of things that other people might've considered necessities, they had formed a bond that neither of them could have expected when they first came to Golden to bid on the house.

Mallory's thoughts were interrupted by a loud knocking on the door followed by an impatient trilling of the old doorbell. Figuring it was either a delivery man or a nosy neighbor wanting to know how long the racket was going to continue, she went down the hallway through the foyer and to the door, opening it without checking to see who was outside.

Her mouth literally fell open. She could feel her jaw just about touching her breastbone. It just could not be, and yet it was! For a moment she seriously wondered if perhaps her mother, ever the practical joker, was pulling a prank of epic proportions on her.

She dismissed that thought quickly, though, even her mother was not this prankish.

Jim's cold eyes took in her bedraggled appearance and disapproval practically shone out of his entire thin face. "Mallory, how are you?"

"What the hell are you doing here?"

"I've had a little time to think things through and I've decided that perhaps I was hasty."

She blinked, she blinked again. Her jaw left her breastbone but only because her teeth clenched together over some words that she was sure would stun the elderly lady walking her dog past the house. It took her a few moments to regain her composure long enough to speak and when she did her voice was deceptively pleasant.

"Jim, I'm not sure why you're here and quite frankly I don't care. However, you're interrupting me in the middle of something very important and I don't really have time to talk to you so if you don't mind I'm going to get back to what I was doing."

She tried to close the door but he stuck out one foot and kept the door from closing. Mallory took note of the fleeting expression of pain that crossed his face when the door edge met his foot. She wasn't sure if the pain was due to the heavy door meeting his foot or if he was in pain at the thought of the scuff that would be on his Italian leather.

"Mallory, do not be hasty. I know you're angry with me and you have every right to be. I would never invalidate your feelings by suggesting that perhaps you should have gotten over them by now."

"Then don't. Quite honestly, Jim I have gotten over them and you too. So why don't you take yourself back to Chicago and see if you can't find yourself another woman to fuck over?"

His face took on a wounded expression. "Is that how you honestly feel? Do you honestly feel as if I harmed you?"

"I think you would've liked to have harmed me, Jim. Only, I figured you out easily. I figured out that you weren't worth my heart much less any damage done to it. There are a lot of things in life that are worth that, but you are not one of them."

She took a step back, meaning to swing the door shut but again his foot prevented it from doing so. His face took on a slightly menacing expression as he said in a voice colder than any she had ever heard him use, "Has it ever occurred to you that most of that was your fault?"

"Is that why you came here, Jim? Did you come here just to unburden yourself of your guilt and to make yourself feel better by placing all the blame on me?"

"I came here because you refuse to process this whole thing with me."

"Process the whole thing with you, Jim? I'm sorry. I don't quite understand what you're trying to say."

His voice was petulant, whiny even. "You left before I could collect my thoughts and get back with you and have a conversation with you about the whole situation. You just up and left and you didn't even bother leaving a forwarding address or anything else."

"You are a piece of work." Mallory was so angry she was shaking all over and her hair was standing up on the back of her neck. "You changed your phone number and you moved out of our house and I don't recall you having left a forwarding address either. What did you expect? That I would still be sitting there in that damn apartment waiting for you to come back, to process with me?

"Do you know what I think you're trying to say to me right now, Jim? I think you are trying to say to me that you want to scream and yell and attempt to make me feel guilty. I think you want to try to manipulate the situation and while I'm not sure for what purpose, I know there is some purpose to this. Why don't you just spill it out right here, right now?"

"You don't have to behave this way."

"You didn't have to be such an asshole."

"Do you know how hard I looked for you?"

"No and I don't care."

Blake spoke up from behind her. "Mallory, is there something going on here that you need my help with?" He seriously doubted it, in fact he was a little worried but not about her, about the safety of the man standing in the doorway. Mallory had an expression on her face that said she would like to kick him in a place both soft and vulnerable.

"No, nothing at all, Blake. Oh wait, Blake meet Jim— my ex—from Chicago."

Oh, so this was the guy. What had she seen in him? He was thin and sallow. He looked as if he spent two hours a day brushing his hair in just that perfect direction and if his clothes had any more starch in them they could've walked away entirely unaided from his body.

"It's nice to meet you."

Jim bared his teeth at him as if he were a feral little dog. "Are you the reason why my fiancée ran away from Chicago?"

Mallory spat out, "You are the reason I left Chicago. You broke up with me, moved out of our apartment, told me that you needed space and time and that you didn't think you were ready to commit to me and that I was a lousy cook. I hardly think Blake had anything to do with it."

Blake was getting a little tired of this man on his doorstep. It was obvious that Mallory was far past the point of being aggravated by Jim. Before he could make a move to do anything about that, the house took that long breath and Blake grabbed Mallory, wrapping her body into his with one strong arm while shouting at Jim, "You better run for your life, mister. I think the house is a little pissed at you."

All the color leached from Jim's face. He bent over double and Blake heard a funny little crackle that he could've sworn—and sincerely hoped—was caused by the starch in the crotch of his slacks. If that wasn't the starch, the man was in a lot more trouble than Blake had originally assumed. He didn't like the guy simply because of what he had done to Mallory but any guy could sympathize with the dude who just had a ghost kick him in the crotch with a whole house behind its weight.

The squeaky little cry that issued from Jim's lips was eerily like the squeak of a mouse and Mallory looked around and said, "Gee, thanks, Ms. Lewis."

The men who had been working in the house had heard the confrontation and come to see what was going on. They were standing in the hallway behind Mallory and Blake and all of them were obviously empathetic to Jim's injury. One even dropped his hands to his crotch and looked around suspiciously as if he were afraid that he might be next.

Blake said, "I don't think the house likes you, Jim. If this house doesn't like you then you don't stand a chance and if I were you I think I'd hit the bricks before I got myself another hard kick."

Jim managed to squeal out, "What's just happened? I'm going to sue you!"

Blake and Mallory were saved from having to answer by one of the men behind them saying, "I don't think you can sue a ghost but you're welcome to try. Everyone knows this house is haunted and old Ms. Lewis, well, she was a sly one." He directed a look at the ceiling and added, "No offense meant."

Mallory watched Jim hobble down the stairs and the walkway towards the street. Blake's arm remained around her and she relaxed into his body, wondering exactly what it was that had brought Jim to the house on this day.

That question was answered pretty quickly though when her mother pulled up into the driveway next door and Jim spotted her. Cara gave him a friendly little wave and called out, "Did you enjoy your visit?"

"Your mother is quite vindictive when she wants to be, isn't she?" Blake asked as Mallory began to giggle.

"It seems that way. I guess that's a warning to you not to get on her bad side."

"I think I am more afraid of my grandmother than your mother but God knows I don't want to make either of them angry."

"Come on, sweetie, let's get back to work. I want this house done by Christmas."

Blake said, "Me too. I think this is going to be the best Christmas in history and I want everything to be perfect."

Chapter 7

The seasons had changed. Winter had blown in on its usual blustery gales. The live oaks that had given the house its name had shed most of their leaves but not all. The long strands of Spanish moss had died, and fallen from the limbs. Blake had raked up giant piles of it and they had used it and small branches to create beautiful homemade wreaths that hung from the oak trees, beckoning visitors onward toward the house. The grass was going dormant but the azaleas and the red camellia bushes bloomed, bringing bright splashes of color to the yard.

Gray Oaks was lit up with Christmas lights and the sound of laughter rang out in the rooms. Blake had just finished putting a giant star on the top of the huge artificial tree he had brought home the day before and the smell of cinnamon and roasting meat filled the air.

Mallory came into the living room with a cup of hot mulled wine and passed it to him. He looked down at it and asked, "Should I be having this?"

"Of course you should, silly. I'm the one that's pregnant, not you."

"Now this is true." He wrapped an arm around her waist, letting his fingers stroke her slightly rounded belly. "Wow, would you look at this place? It looks so different."

"Yes, it does."

The floors were repaired, the walls painted and the ceilings gleamed with fresh molding and light fixtures. The furniture had been replaced but the paintings of Shannon and her family remained, and alongside them hung pictures of Blake and his paternal family including his father. A wedding photo of Mallory and Blake was now on the wall too.

There was a hush in the air, a quiet expectancy that neither of them could fathom but still felt. Blake asked, "What time is everyone coming over?"

"In about an hour. I have the table all set already. Thank God my mother agreed to cook. I think I'm getting better though, that Hamburger Helper I made last night didn't taste bad at all."

Blake managed to say with a perfectly straight face, "No, it wasn't bad at all."

"You liar. You only ate it because you were starving and my mother would not let you have any more cookies."

"You got me, I can't deny it. It was not that your Hamburger Helper was bad, sweetheart; it's just that your mother's cookies are so dang good. It's like they are magic cookies."

"I said that Hamburger Helper wasn't that bad, I never said that it was good. It was about halfway between good and bad. You don't have to lie, you know."

"Okay, maybe next time we should try actually cooking the noodles all the way through." He ducked under her mock blows, laughing as he came back around her and captured her, pressing her into his arms. He kissed her again, a slow and soft kiss that made her whole body respond in a way she had never imagined possible when she was with Jim. "I love you whether your noodles are raw or cooked."

"I love you too," Mallory replied.

Blake ruffled her flame-hued hair. "I have to admit the best thing I ever did was try to buy this house."

"Maybe it was fate," Mallory suggested.

Blake said, "You know, I think it was. I just wish that they had had the chance to be as happy as we are."

Oh, I wish the same thing. It's so lonely here, George, even with these two beautiful people to light up the house. I miss you so, I think I miss you more every day. I'm staying here though, for as long as it takes. I said I would be here for you and I will be but I do wish you would hurry, George.

I've waited so long for our wedding, I've waited so long to touch your face and to put my hand in yours. To feel the press of your lips against mine once again. I know for us time isn't the same, when you step out of your body and become spirit, time doesn't matter anymore and I know you have no idea how long I've been waiting but it's been so long, George.

I could use a Christmas gift, George, I could use some blessings this year. That girl lit candles in every window this year, did you see them, George? They're burning and are not just burning so that the people who are still alive and who are coming to this house tonight can find their way in here but also that you can find your way home. Is that light enough, George, will you ever make it home to me?

"I have an idea."

Blake asked, "What kind of idea?"

"Let's call him."

Blake cocked an eyebrow at her. "I don't think it's as simple as picking up the phone and saying hey, George, you're a little late, old buddy."

"No, but what if he just needs a little more guidance? Let's try it. I know it sounds silly, but just humor me, will you? Come on, just yell out his name… Like this." Mallory sucked in a huge breath and then released it in a loud and piercing cry, "George! George, come home, George!"

Blake did feel silly. While he absolutely believed that his grandmother was still in the house, he wasn't so sure yelling at a dead man would help bring him to her, but if Mallory was going to engage in this little bit of foolishness then so was he. He was her husband and he would always have her back. He would always help her in any endeavor, no matter how silly it seemed. He raised his own voice, yelling in unison with her, "George! George, are you there? George, come home!"

After a few more minutes of shouting Blake was ready to give up. He swallowed down most of the cup of mulled wine to relieve the dryness in his throat that the shouting caused and said, "I'm sorry, hon. I just don't think he's going to show. Maybe he already crossed over, maybe he couldn't help it. Maybe he just got sucked up like the people do when they get stuck in an alien tractor beam."

"Are you comparing going to heaven with being sucked up into an alien spaceship?" Indignation was written all over Mallory's expression. "And on Christmas!"

He tweaked her cute little upturned nose, "I would never dare. I was making an analogy. But think about it, Mallory. Maybe that is exactly what happened. Maybe because he died in battle he got taken straight up and he never had a chance to make his way home again. Maybe it isn't George that needs to come home, maybe it's Shannon that needs to go home."

Just then the front door blew open, bringing in a gust of wintry air and the scent of hyacinth mixed with lilies. The wind tore along the hallway and Blake and Mallory looked at each other, their eyes wide.

Blake asked, "Is that…"

"I think so," Mallory breathed.

"Oh, there you are, what took you so long?"

That question was spoken aloud and the voice asking was young, strong and clear. Blake pushed Mallory behind him in a protective gesture that made her laugh and say, "It's fine, silly. I want to see too!"

There wasn't anything to see, really. The paintings on the wall trembled and the photograph of Blake's father tilted then straightened as if a loving hand had set it at a precise angle.

They both felt it. They had always felt Shannon, although they had never really been aware that they were actually sensing her. Her presence drifted past them almost like an eddy of air. Blake felt fingers that rippled through his hair, sensing that they came from somewhere beside him, but were not Shannon's.

As quickly as that touch landed on his head it was gone. The wind died down and the smell of flowers grew stronger, stronger and then the wind gusted up again, running in the opposite direction—out of the house.

The door shut, but quietly and the house settled around them, no less bright and warm than it had been before but yet they could feel the difference. Shannon was gone. George had finally been able to find his way back to her and they had gone wherever it was that lovers went after they were reunited after many years apart.

Mallory's eyes filled with tears and she saw Blake trying to hide his own. Men, they always thought they had to be so strong!

"I think that was the best Christmas gift we could have gotten," Mallory said softly. "It lets us know love always lasts, doesn't it?"

"It does," Blake said. "But I have no intentions of being separated from you, darling, not ever."

"Nor I you."

He pointed upward, "Mistletoe."

"I hope you do know that I would kiss you without that being there."

"I do but since it is hanging up there in the doorway I intend to take advantage of it."

Their laughter rang out onto the street and Shannon Lewis paused, her hand securely in George's, and looked back at her house. "I think Gray Oaks will be a far happier place for the next hundred years, George, what do you think?"

"I think it's found its new family." He gave her a long kiss and said, "Come on—we don't want to be late for our wedding, do we?"

Shannon laughed and allowed herself to be pulled off the earthly plane and into one where the love that she had held onto in life lived on and on forever.

About Kate Goldman

In childhood I observed a huge love between my mother and father and promised myself that one day I would meet a man whom I would fall in love with head over heels. At the age of 16, I wrote my first romance story that was published in a student magazine and was read by my entire neighborhood. I enjoy writing romance stories that readers can turn into captivating imaginary movies where characters fall in love, overcome difficult obstacles, and participate in best adventures of their lives. Most of the time you can find me reading a great fiction book in a cozy armchair, writing a romance story in a hammock near the ocean, or traveling around the world with my beloved husband.

One Last Thing...

If you believe that *In Love With a Haunted House* is worth sharing, would you spend a minute to let your friends know about it?

If this book lets them have a great time, they will be enormously grateful to you – as will I.

Kate

www.KateGoldmanBooks.com

Made in the USA
San Bernardino, CA
18 May 2019